Sherlock Holmes and the

Molly-Boy Murders

By

Margaret Walsh

Paperback ISBN 978-1-78705-474-5
ePub ISBN 978-1-78705-475-2
PDF ISBN 978-1-78705-476-9

Published by MX Publishing
335 Princess Park Manor, Royal Drive,
London, N11 3GX
www.mxpublishing.co.uk

Cover design by Brian Belanger

Chapter One

I take up my pen once again to recount an extraordinary case solved by my good friend, Mr. Sherlock Holmes, although, given the nature of the events that I will recount, it is exceedingly unlikely that this manuscript will ever be published. Indeed, I gave my word to one of the principals that such a thing would not occur. But it behooves me as a witness to the events to record them for posterity.

It was a cool spring day, several months after the dreadful events of Whitechapel horrified London, and indeed, the whole country, and several months before the ghastly events at Baskerville Hall. The sun was endeavouring to burn away the light fog that enveloped our part of the city.

Holmes and I were enjoying a leisurely breakfast when Inspector Lestrade arrived. I described him in my first volume of our adventures as a sallow, rat-faced, little man. He was not rat-faced as such, more that his moustache tended to twitch like a rodent's whiskers on occasion. It was as fine a moustache as any that graced the philtrum of a Mayfair gentleman.

It was this case that persuaded my friend that Lestrade was truly dependable, steadfast and discreet. It was also this case that lead to Lestrade being included in the denouement of the dreadful events on Dartmoor.

On this particular morning the normally unshakeable inspector was white-faced, his moustache twitching almost uncontrollably. I took one look at him and hastened for the brandy. Holmes assisted our visitor to a chair. "What on Earth is wrong, Lestrade? I have never seen you so shaken," Holmes said. Concern shaded his tone in a way few people ever heard.

Lestrade took the brandy I offered him, balancing it on his knee briefly as he strove to control the slight shake of his hand. He sipped it gently for a moment. "We need your help, Mr. Holmes. We have got another." His moustache gave a violent twitch.

"Another what, may I ask?" Holmes' voice was gentler than it would normally be under the circumstances.

Lestrade took a fortifying gulp of the brandy. "Another Ripper."

"What?" I sank down in my own chair, aghast at the news. The previous summer and autumn had seen a spate of the most terrible, horrendously violent, killings. Women gutted like pigs in the streets of London's East End. The newspapers had gone into a frenzy seldom seen before, and the people of London had been left shocked and traumatized.

Holmes' offer of assistance had been rudely rebuffed by the then-Commissioner of Police, Sir Charles Warren. An unlikeable man with an inflated sense of his own importance, and totally lacking in anything even faintly resembling common sense. He had resigned in disgrace and been replaced with James Monro. A man much admired by the men who served under him.

Holmes settled back in his chair, steepling his fingers beneath his chin. "Tell me," he said.

"We found a corpse. A young man, well, a boy really. Found naked, throat slit, and the body mutilated." Lestrade drank more brandy, looked at me hopefully, and held out the glass for a refill. I obliged. Lestrade sipped the brandy slowly. "We cannot identify him. No one knows who he is. This was about three weeks ago. Then today..." Lestrade swallowed convulsively "...we got another one."

Holmes leaned forward. "Where is the corpse?"

"At the Royal London." Lestrade took a deep breath. "Warren was wrong not to want your help during last year's unpleasantness. But God help me, we simply cannot afford another Ripper panic so soon. Mr. Holmes, will you help?"

"Of course I will." Holmes looked at me, and I nodded. "We both will."

Lestrade put his glass on the table. "I have a cab waiting downstairs. Will you come with me now?"

In answer, we both got up, fetched our coats, and followed Lestrade down the stairs. Our agreement to assist appeared to have assuaged his fears. The Lestrade that preceded us was almost his old self again. Not the white-faced, trembling wreck that had entered our flat such a short time before.

In the cab, Holmes asked for more detail. Lestrade obliged. "The first body was found in an alley off Piccadilly. A carter found it. Nearly threw up on it, poor sod. This one was found by a police constable patrolling Victoria Embankment. The constable is in nearly the same state as the carter."

I was somewhat startled. It takes something fairly gruesome to upset the strong stomachs of such stalwarts as carters and police officers.

Holmes sat back in his seat, content to wait until we reached our destination to ask more questions

The Royal London Hospital, being situated in Whitechapel, tended to garner more than its fair share of victims of violent death. After the previous year's killings, it was slowly becoming the place where Scotland Yard dumped its more ghastly corpses for examination.

Our trip to the Royal London was swift, the traffic on the streets being unusually light for the time of day. On arrival, Lestrade led us down to the morgue.

The police surgeon, Dr. Thomas Bond, looked up as we entered. He raised an eyebrow.

"Assistance, Lestrade?"

Lestrade gave a tight smile. "Doctor Bond, may I introduce Mr. Sherlock Holmes and Doctor John Watson."

A small smile spread across Bond's face. His was not a face given to easy smiles. Bond was a firm-featured, square-jawed man, who would no doubt be described as handsome by the ladies of his acquaintance. He had served briefly with the Prussian military and served as police surgeon for A Division through several of their most trying cases. Most notably the Whitechapel murders, the Battersea mystery, and the Thames torso killings.

Bond nodded in my direction. "Not a man to be disturbed by our corpse, then." He gestured for me to step up to the table.

I walked to Dr. Bond's side and looked down at the young man laid out upon the stained wooden table. The scent of carbolic made my nostrils twitch, and the smell of old blood and viscera was awakening memories of Afghanistan.

The boy was so young. He looked to be around fourteen or fifteen years of age, fair complexion and blonde hair. His throat was slit almost from ear to ear. Blood flecked the ends of his hair and the base of his throat. I froze, shocked. The young man had been mutilated. His genitalia completely removed. A bulging in his cheeks told me exactly where they had been placed. I felt ill. For a moment the room swirled around me. Visions of Afghani atrocities danced in my memory. Briefly I felt the urge to run away and hide.

"Watson?" Holmes' voice held curiosity and concern. He walked up and stood beside me. "Hmmm."

I found my voice. "Cause of death is possibly the wound to the throat. The genitals were certainly removed after death."

"Cause of death 'possibly' the throat wound?" Holmes voice held a slight note of challenge.

I stiffened and glared at him, which, knowing Holmes as I did, had probably been his intention. "Lestrade, was there much blood where the body was found?" I asked.

"No, there was not. Just a small amount around the wound."

"The lack of blood from the wound, Holmes, combined with the slight congestion of the face suggests that the cause of death was in all probability asphyxia."

Doctor Bond nodded and raised the corpse's eyelid. He handed me a magnifying glass and I bent to examine the eyeball. "Ahhhh."

"Enlightening as always, Watson."

"There are flecks of blood in the eyeball. Petechial hemorrhage it is called. The result of either strangulation or asphyxia from having a cloth, or even just a strong hand, pinch off the breath. It is likely then that the heart had ceased to beat when his throat was slit, and his genitals were removed. Most probably with a razor or a butcher's knife."

Lestrade spoke up. "Why not a scalpel? Could the killer be a doctor?"

Holmes snorted. "Really, Lestrade, do not tell me that you believed that rubbish about the Whitechapel killer being a medical man?"

The look Lestrade threw Holmes was poisonous in the extreme.

I shook my head. "Take a look for yourself. The genitals were removed with one slice. A scalpel blade is too fine. It would take two or more strokes. This was done cleanly in one. So either a butcher's knife or a broad bladed razor is responsible."

Doctor Bond hummed his agreement. "What do you make of the torso, Doctor Watson?"

The body of the young man showed a deformity that should have been familiar to me, but I could not place it. I frowned. Holmes had his own glass out, studying the body closely. He handed me the glass, "Look at the base of the ribcage. There are marks. Not ones I am familiar with."

I took the glass from him and looked closely. The torso was almost feminine, with flesh pushed up and contorted above the ribcage, and the ribcage itself deformed with the ribs being compressed into almost a tubular shape. Deep red marks scored the skin at the pelvis and at the base of the ribcage. I noted absently a small mole upon the lad's right shoulder. I frowned again, searching my memory. Then it came to me and I blushed.

"What is it, Watson?" Holmes noted my blush, but did not comment, much to my relief.

"This poor lad is not exactly a lad."

"Whatever do you mean?" Holmes tilted his head to one side, giving me a slightly irritated, though inquiring, look.

"The medical profession does not have a proper name for them. At least, not yet. But this young man has spent much of his time dressed in women's clothing. The deformity of the torso and the marks upon it show that he has been wearing a corset that was tight laced for most of the time."

"Tight laced?" Holmes leaned forward with the expression of avid curiosity and interest that he wore when confronted with new information that might prove to be of use to him at some future time. It came to me that Holmes genuinely would not know about tight lacing, or even the intricacies of a normally laced corset. Any time I had seen him impersonate women, and he had done so on several occasions to my knowledge, Holmes had been dressed as woman from the working classes or lower. Women who could not afford a corset, or possibly had never even seen one, except discarded on the second-hand clothing stalls of Petticoat Lane.

"Most women wear corsets firmly laced to give them a more pleasing shape and to support the back. However, some women, mostly upper class, and middle class with aspirations, tight lace. The idea is to create the perfect female form. The ideal waist in these women's minds is about thirteen inches."

My friend frowned.

"The average circumference of a woman's waist is about twenty-six inches," I explained. "The laces are slowly tightened over a period of time to shrink the waist ten or more inches. It does dreadful damage to their internal organs. Infertility is a major problem."

Holmes appeared to absorb the information. "And what about our corpse, Watson?"

"A sexual pervert?" asked Lestrade.

Doctor Bond shook his head. "Not necessarily, Inspector. There have been cases where young men have grown up feeling that they are in actuality young women."

"Boulton and Parks," my friend said softly.

Bond nodded. "Boulton in particular," he said.

Lestrade frowned.

Holmes tone was cold. "Surely you remember it, Lestrade? It was something of a cause célèbre. Two young men who dressed as women, charged with 'conspiring to incite others to commit unnatural acts.' It was hardly the police force's most shining hour."

Lestrade's brow cleared. "Of course, Fanny and Stella. That was pretty much a disaster all round. And before my time, I might add."

"Indeed," said Bond, his voice loaded with disdain, "…and in the case of Ernest Boulton, also known as Stella, he had dressed as a girl from a very young age. The examining doctors speculated that the two of them were some form of hermaphrodite. They could not even agree if the youngsters had been engaged in unnatural intercourse or not." His tone implied his extremely low opinion of the medical skills of the said doctors.

Privately I agreed with him. Ernest Boulton and Frederick Parks had been treated with the utmost cruelty and coldness. To the extent of being intimately examined by multiple doctors. Then dragged into court clad in bedraggled feminine attire to face derision in the court and in the eye of the public.

"In the case of these young men, including our corpse, they want a feminine figure. So when they wear female clothing, they tight lace as a matter of course," I continued.

Lestrade looked down at the young man on the table. "So why kill him?"

Doctor Bond sighed. "There could be many reasons. I noticed when I examined him that his anal sphincter was extremely loose."

The inspector shot the Doctor Bond a sharp look. "He was a whore?"

"There is a high balance of probability that he was."

"A disgruntled customer perhaps, who did not realize what he was buying?"

"That explains one corpse, Lestrade, but not two, said Holmes. "A man may be fooled once, but a second time is suggestive of planning. It is also uncommon for men take large knives with them when they are planning on entertaining a whore. Not unless they have a vastly different idea of what constitutes entertainment than other men."

Lestrade's face contorted into a slightly wry expression, acknowledging my friend's argument. "You make a valid point, Mr. Holmes. He set out with a deliberate intent to kill." Lestrade's expression turned mournful. "It does look like we have another Ripper on our hands after all."

One thing was puzzling me. "Where would he get the clothing?" I asked. "It is not as if a lad can go to a dressmaker to be fitted."

Lestrade answered my query. "There are houses, Doctor, run by women who provide lodging and clothing for young men such as this one. They arrive dressed as men, and go out on the street dressed as women."

"We shall need to talk to some of them if we are to find out who is doing this. Come, Watson." Holmes turned away abruptly, obviously intending to leave.

"Where are we going, Holmes?" I asked.

Holmes turned back, and gave me an irritated look, as if annoyed I even needed to ask the question. "To one of these houses Lestrade mentioned. We need to chat with some gentlemen whores, and their keepers. We shall need you too, Inspector."

"Me?" Lestrade raised his eyebrows.

"Of course, you obviously know of the existence of at least one of these houses. Your tone of voice told me that much. We shall need your knowledge, not to mention an introduction to the madams." He turned around and strode out of the door.

Lestrade and I shared a look of exasperation before striding after him. I turned back, quickly shook Doctor Bond's hand, and hurried to catch up. The game, as Holmes would say, was afoot.

Chapter Two

Lestrade gave the cabbie an address in Marylebone, not too far from our lodgings, and we settled comfortably inside.

The Inspector had an expression on his face reminiscent of a man biting into an orange and discovering that it was a lemon. "You gentlemen are in for a rare treat. We are going to meet Gertrude Swindon – spinster of the parish, purveyor of lodgings to young single men, possible bawd, and the one dragon Saint George missed."

"Possible bawd?" Holmes queried.

Lestrade sighed. "The lady is too clever for us. No sexual intercourse takes place on the premises, and no incriminating female garments could be found in the boys' rooms."

"Then how do you know she is a bawd?" I asked. It appeared to me that Lestrade was guilty of the sort of guess work that infuriated Holmes.

Lestrade grimaced. "There is a room in the house. A very fine room with wardrobes full of female apparel. Also in the room are other clothes best described as costumes. When the house was raided, we were informed that her young men indulge in amateur theatricals. We could not prove that this was not the case. So Mrs. Swindon was discharged without conviction, and we were rapped over the knuckles by the magistrate at Bow Street." The grimace turned into an outright scowl.

The cab bustled on, headed towards our part of the city. It finally turned into Cleveland Street, going past the former workhouse, now an annex of the Middlesex hospital.

We alighted in front of a modest house of four floors, including a basement. It was clean and tidy, and gave no sign of what allegedly lurked within.

Lestrade took a deep breath, squared his shoulders, and marched up the steps to ring the bell, looking for all the world like a soldier going into battle.

The door was opened by a woman who reminded me, fleetingly, of Mrs. Hudson. She was straight-backed, with tight chestnut curls drawn back into a loose chignon, and deep blue eyes that looked squarely out at the world. The lady also had an aristocratic aquiline nose that she looked down along towards Lestrade as though he were a piece of flotsam left behind by the tide.

"Inspector Lestrade, to what do I owe the somewhat dubious pleasure of your company?" She looked past him to us, and her upper lip curled. "And the company of your friends." She made it sound as though we were drunken debauchers, rather than a detective from Scotland Yard, a consulting detective, and a respectable doctor.

Holmes walked up the stairs and extended his hand. "My dear Mrs. Swindon, may we enter your fine premises? We need to talk."

"We can talk as well upon the doorstep, sir."

"It is not fitting to discuss murder in so public a place."

"Murder?" The look the lady gave my friend was dark. "Very well. Inspector," she turned to Lestrade, who was leaning against the railing, apparently sulking. "You may bring your friends inside, but make it brief. I have no desire for your company for any longer than I must."

"I assure you, madam, that the feeling is mutual!"

She stepped back, and opened the door wider, allowing the three of us to enter. As the door closed behind us, she turned to my friend. "Now sir, what is this nonsense about murder?"

"No nonsense, madam. Two young men have been found with their throats slit and bodies mutilated. They had something in common with your lodgers."

"And what would that be?" Gertrude Swindon all but sneered the question at Holmes.

"An interest in amateur theatricals."

Her lips twitched at that, but she remained silent.

"Have any of your lodgers gone missing?" Lestrade asked.

"That is none of your business, Inspector." Her tone was cold enough to freeze brass.

It was the last straw for me.

"Have you no compassion, woman?" The words burst from my mouth. "Two young men brutally cut down. Are you so devoid of any desire other than to protect your sordid little business?" I strove to keep my tone civil, but the memory of the dreadful corpse I had just seen was powering my words, no doubt leading me to make a spectacle of myself.

She opened her mouth to reply, but I kept going. "We have just come from the morgue at the Royal London. Should we take you there, madam, to see that poor lad, fair hair tousled and streaked with the blood from his slit throat? Someone must be missing him. Did he have a sweetheart who would kiss the mole upon his right shoulder?"

I heard Lestrade mutter to Holmes "I had not realized the good doctor was a romantic at heart."

I ignored them both, my emotions too engaged in the unfeeling woman before me.

A sharp intake of breath stopped my tirade. I looked up. Standing at the foot of the interior staircase was a very young man. He had brown curly hair and anxious brown eyes. His voice, when he spoke, was low and soft, with an almost musical quality. "That sounds like Molly. She did not return home last night."

I noted the use of the female name and pronoun. I saw both Holmes and Lestrade take note of it as well.

Holmes moved towards him. "You knew her well?"

"She had the room across the landing from mine."

Holmes looked at him in silence for a moment. When he next spoke, his voice was gentle. "Will you come to the morgue with us, lad, to see if the poor unfortunate is Molly?"

The lad swallowed hard, shot a glance at Gertrude Swindon, whose face was expressionless, and nodded his agreement.

We sat in silence on the trip back to the morgue. The boy had said his name was Daniel Watts, but that is all he would say before lapsing into silence. His mood affected ours, and we all stared gloomily out into the crowded streets, or sank deeply into our own thoughts.

Once at the mortuary, Lestrade wasted no time in chivying the attendant into opening the drawer that held the latest victim. The attendant was a dark-haired, surly man, with a moustache that made him resemble a small terrier carrying a dead rat, and he was reluctant to do Lestrade's bidding. Though a few sharp words from the little detective soon had him dragging the drawer open, grumbling to himself all the while.

Daniel had hung back by the door. His eyes were wide with fear, and I could see his nostrils flare at the unpleasant smells that hung in the room in an almost visible fashion. I could understand his apprehension. A morgue is not a place for those of a gentle or nervous disposition.

Holmes stood beside Lestrade at the open drawer, and beckoned the lad to join them. With great reluctance, he approached them. I could see he was regretting agreeing to come with us.

Daniel took one look at the face, and turned away. "That is Molly. She was born David Clutterbuck." His voice was choked with misery.

Having been persuaded to be helpful, the attendant now came forward with a photograph he had taken from a drawer in the desk that lay against one of the walls. He handed it to Lestrade in silence. Lestrade looked at it. "This is the first victim. Daniel, do you know this person?" He held out the photograph. It showed a young man, slightly older than Daniel and David. His face less than peaceful in death.

Daniel glanced at the photograph. "I did not know her, but Molly did. She was known as Nancy. They had several friends in common." He looked at the floor. When he looked up again, he showed a different demeanor from the shy young lad of before. "Promise me you will find who did this." His fury was palpable. "Molly did not deserve to die like that. And I am sure Nancy did not either."

"We will do our best, Daniel. We have somewhere to start now." Lestrade handed the photograph back to the attendant. "Thank you, Hooper." The man nodded and walked away, placing the photograph back where he had obtained it.

We returned Daniel to Cleveland Street, Lestrade went back to Scotland Yard, and Holmes and I returned to Baker Street to begin our hunt for the killer.

It was several days before we had any information to work with.

The evening was still cool enough to need a fire, and Holmes and I were seated comfortably before it. Outside the window, wisps of mist danced in the air, obviously looking to settle in for the night.

Holmes went over what we had learned so far, from both Lestrade, and from the streets. Holmes' Baker Street Irregulars, as he called them, were singularly useful in gathering all sorts of information.

"The second victim, David Clutterbuck, also known as Molly, has been tracked down by Lestrade," Holmes said. "He had a widowed mother in Slough, who has been told only that her son has been killed. There was no need to distress her with the details."

"Lestrade sometimes has more compassion than we give him credit for," I said. "Indeed, Watson. David was sixteen years old and had moved away from home two years ago when he got taken on as a shop clerk at a haberdashers on the Strand. That is the extent of the news from our good Inspector."

Holmes' tone told me he had still more information.

"But you have news from other sources?"

"You are becoming very observant, Watson."

"You are becoming very obvious, Holmes. Your Irregulars have been out and about?"

"That they have. The lads know those that frequent the seamier side of this fair city once the sun sets."

"They have learned something of interest?" I asked.

"They have learned several things, both useful and interesting. They have found little about Nancy. No other name is known. She plied her trade in several of the little alleyways off Piccadilly. If Nancy had a pimp, the boys could not find out who bore that honour, dubious as it is."

I could not forebear snorting derisively. We had run into a few pimps in some of our previous cases, and none of them could be described as honourable. Scrofulous, vicious, and avaricious were the descriptions that came most readily to mind.

Holmes continued. "According to what the boys learned, Nancy was in business for herself. She had been on the streets for around three years. It really is remarkable that she survived that long, the streets being what they are. David, or Molly if you prefer, had only been working for about a year. The two of them were friends. They often drank together in local pubs, and loitered in front of the theatres and dance halls from Piccadilly to the Strand whilst they sought custom. They occasionally ventured down to the Embankment as well. Wiggins tells me that they had several clients in common."

"You think the killer may be one of their clients?" I asked.

"It is a distinct possibility, Watson, but not one I wish to entertain until I have more data. I have warned you before of the dangers of theorizing without facts." Holmes gave me a wintry little smile.

"Indeed. It is, however, difficult to entertain any possibility except that we have a new version of the Whitechapel killer on the loose." I brooded silently for a while. "I really cannot understand the coldness of that woman, Swindon. A young man who lodged in her house was murdered and she did not care."

Holmes shook his head. "My dear Watson, you saw only what she wanted you to see."

"Whatever do you mean?" I asked, more than a little cross with his tone.

"You saw a cold, unfeeling, woman. I saw someone very different. I saw a woman whose eyes were red from weeping, and who had lines of worry deepening across her brow. You allowed the cold, harsh, exterior to stop you from looking closer, and that, my friend, is exactly what she wanted you to do. Gertrude Swindon cares, Watson, probably more than is advisable for a woman in her position to do. You need to learn to look beyond the obvious. To see the things other people do not wish you to see."

I sat back, brows creased in thought, attempting to formulate a reply.

Mrs. Hudson entered with a telegram in her hand. "Just delivered, Mr. Holmes."

He rose to his feet and took the telegram from her, tore it open, and scanned the contents."

"Quickly, Watson, we are needed."

I also rose to my feet, and grabbed for my coat. "Has there been another killing?" I asked.

"Yes. Lestrade requests our presence."

Down the stairs we went and hailed a cab.

We traveled again in silence to the morgue we had so recently visited. The mist thickened into fog as we approached Whitechapel. Swirling in off the Thames, it seemed almost alive, and deeply malevolent.

Lestrade was out in front of the building waiting for us. He stood beside the door, shoulders hunched, as though the weight of the world rested upon them.

"We have got another, but something is off about this one," Lestrade said, as soon as we had stepped from the cab.

The inspector looked weary and baffled.

Holmes and I followed him inside.

Doctor Bond was once again officiating. He nodded a greeting, and gestured to the table, wiping his hands as he turned away. Holmes and I stood, one on either side of the table.

Holmes looked across at Lestrade, who stood just inside the door, reluctant to come any further. "You are correct. This killing is superficially the same, but there are points of difference. This is a man in perhaps his late twenties or early thirties. The other two were mere boys."

I frowned over the corpse. "He has been wearing a corset too. You can see the marks, but there is no deformity from tight lacing. He has, however, been mutilated like the others."

Lestrade pushed away from the door frame he had been leaning against, and moved to stand beside me. "He was found on Victoria Embankment. Just the same as David Clutterbuck."

Doctor Bond looked up from where he was washing his arms. "He most definitely was not a whore. There was no looseness, or wear and tear, of the anus that I could note."

Lestrade frowned down at the corpse, as if he expected it to speak to him. "Who are you?" he asked softly.

We all jumped a little when a voice answered "Jeremiah Bradstreet."

I turned towards the door and saw Mycroft Holmes standing there. I stared at him in shock. It must be something very grave indeed to make Mycroft break from his daily routine.

Mycroft walked across to us, stood next to his brother, and looked down at the corpse. "Jeremiah Bradstreet was supposed to report to me at my office this morning. He never arrived."

Holmes had told me how Mycroft was the one man clearing house of information for the government. In many instances he is the British government. It had simply not occurred to me to wonder how information got to Mycroft.

Mycroft's face held no expression as he gazed down at the corpse. "Someone will have to tell his widow," was all he said after a while.

Lestrade sighed. "Mr. Holmes, I take it you and Dr. Watson know this gentleman?" He waved a hand in Mycroft's general direction. Mycroft Holmes turned a sharp, appraising, look upon Lestrade.

Holmes' lips twitched briefly into an expression that could have been interpreted as a smile. "Inspector Lestrade, this is my brother, Mycroft Holmes, what he does for a living you do not need, or even want, to know."

Lestrade stretched his hand out, and the two men shook hands across the morgue table, and the corpse of Jeremiah Bradstreet. "Notifying the family is police business, sir. If you would like to give me the address, we will go and talk to the widow now."

"We?" asked Mycroft, raising his eyebrows in query.

Lestrade nodded. "Probably a good idea to take the doctor along in case the widow becomes hysterical, and your brother can come along for the ride."

Mycroft's mouth moved into a mirthless smile at Lestrade's sally.

Jeremiah Bradstreet had lived in Putney in a pleasant little house near the river. It was fully dark by the time we arrived. The door was opened by a maid who gaped at us. Lestrade removed his hat, "Is the lady of the house, home, lass?" His voice was gentle.

"Who is it, Mary?"

We looked up to see a young woman, dark-haired and green-eyed, dressed in mourning, coming down the stairs. "Mrs. Bradstreet?" asked Lestrade.

"Yes." She came towards the door. "Who are you gentlemen?"

"I am Inspector Lestrade from Scotland Yard, and this is Mr. Sherlock Holmes, and Doctor John Watson, we have come about your husband, Jeremiah."

Her hand went to her throat. "He did not return home yesterday nor today. Has something happened to him, as well?"

I noted the use of the words "as well" and I could see Holmes doing the same.

Lestrade swallowed convulsively. He was twisting his hat in his hands. There really was not any way to break this dreadful news gently. "I regret to inform you, ma'am, that your husband is dead."

The inspector dropped his hat and leaped forward just in time to catch Mrs. Bradstreet as she slumped into a swoon. Holmes helped hold her up, and they carefully laid her on the floor. I supported her head and shoulders and looked up at the maid. "Mary, is it not?"

"Yes, sir."

"Well Mary, please fetch a glass of water for your mistress."

The girl bobbed a curtsey and scurried away. She returned with the glass of water, and an overbearing ass of a man also dressed in mourning. He was around six feet tall, dark-haired, and with green eyes that darted frantically about, as if in search of an escape route. The man was obviously related to my patient, and the age suggested a sibling.

"What are you doing to my sister? How dare you come into a house of mourning unannounced?" His voice trailed off into a squawk as Lestrade grasped the man's lapels in both hands and, none too gently, pressed him up against the wall beside the door.

"Listen to me, sir," Lestrade invested the last word with a plethora of icy sarcasm. "Your sister fainted when I broke the news to her of her husband's death. I am Inspector Lestrade of Scotland Yard. The last thing she, or any of us needs, is you behaving in such a bumptious and obnoxious manner." Lestrade's voice was a rich palate of anger and contempt.

"Dead? Jeremiah is dead?" His voice was a bleat, like a lost and confused little lamb.

"Ah, so you were indeed listening," said Holmes, from his position kneeling beside Mrs. Bradstreet.

"But how?" the bleating lamb asked.

Holmes left Mrs. Bradstreet in my capable hands, and got to his feet, and went to stand shoulder to shoulder with Lestrade, no doubt in case the man should turn violent.

With Mary's assistance I got Mrs. Bradstreet to her feet and guided her into the front parlour.

Lestrade faced the man squarely, letting go of the shirt front as he did so. "In answer to your question, he was butchered. Like a damn animal."

The man staggered away from the wall. He made a noise somewhere between a hiccough and a sob. "It is too much. First our brother Michael, and now Jeremiah." He shook his head sadly, and walked away into the back of the house.

Holmes and Lestrade stared after him for a moment. Lestrade sighed, and bent down to retrieve his hat, then he and Holmes joined us in the parlour, where Mary had made Mrs.

Bradstreet comfortable on a settee and poured her a small medicinal glass of brandy at my request.

Mrs. Bradstreet, who told us her name was Viola, listened to Lestrade as he explained the circumstances of her husband's death, leaving out as much detail as he could, not wanting to shock her or distress her further.

Mrs. Bradstreet, however, shocked all of us when she asked, "Was he dressed as a woman?"

There was a moment of silence as Holmes, Lestrade, and I absorbed this surprising information.

"How do you know about that?" Holmes asked, his tone gentle.

She nodded. "He told me that it was part of his job."

"A part of his job, you say?" asked Lestrade.

"My husband and my brother, Michael, worked together. I understand that they hunted out England's enemies and sometimes it was necessary for them to pose as husband and wife. Michael was six feet tall. He would never have passed for a woman, but Jeremiah made quite a stately matron, I understand."

"Enemies of England?" Holmes' tone was flat.

"Oh yes. Jeremiah did not want to tell me, but he really had no choice. You see, I found his working clothes; corset, petticoats, and all. I was shocked, and I will tell you sir, that I did not quite believe him when he told me. He had to bring Michael to me to confirm it. They told me I must not say anything to anyone, but now they are both dead, so someone needs to know. To find who killed them. They must both have

27

been killed. At first we thought Michael's death was an accident."

"We?"

"Jeremiah, and Nathaniel, and I. Nathaniel is Michael's twin."

"That must be the obnoxious bully we met in the hallway," Lestrade said, keeping his voice low.

"Nathaniel took the death hard. Michael was found drowned in the Thames three months ago. It was thought he slipped and fell in. His body was found near St. Katherine's Docks"

"Mrs. Bradstreet," Holmes said, "What did your husband and your brother do when they were not hunting out England's enemies? They must have had some daytime occupation." I noted my friend was trying hard to keep the skepticism out of his voice.

Mrs. Bradstreet wiped gently at her eyes with a handkerchief Mary had supplied, and nodded. "They worked for a company in the city. Imperial Exports."

At that moment, the man who had been so rude outside came bursting into the room. "Viola! You should not be alone with these men."

"I am hardly alone, Nathaniel. Mary is here."

"Nevertheless. You have only their word they are who they say they are. They could be madmen, thieves, or worse." He was red-eyed and swaying slightly.

Holmes got to his feet, Lestrade and I followed hurriedly. Lestrade opened his mouth to remonstrate. Holmes looked at him and shook his head. "You will just waste your breath, Lestrade. The stench of whiskey is obvious from where I am standing."

My own nose wrinkled involuntarily as I caught the sour whiff of the spirit Nathaniel had imbibed. Lestrade's twitching moustache signaled his disgust.

Holmes turned to Mrs. Bradstreet. "Allow me to express my deepest regrets for your loss, Mrs. Bradstreet, rest assured that we will do our utmost to find the killer." Holmes sketched a slight bow to the lady, little more than an inclination of the head, and strode out of the room, leaving Lestrade and I to say our goodbyes and hasten after him. Nathaniel Croft continued to sway slowly from side to side and spray nonsense at us.

We caught up with Holmes in the street, climbing into the cab that had waited for us. None of us had felt that we would have much success in obtaining a suitable cab in Putney once full night had fallen.

"Damn it, Holmes. That was a trifle rude." My tone was crisp and curt. I was not happy with Holmes' abrupt departure from the household. Nor was I especially pleased at leaving a drunken sot to care for his grieving sister.

Holmes half turned towards me on the step of the cab, then dropped down to stand beside me. "Rude be damned, Watson. Mycroft is trifling with us."

"What?"

"Imperial Exports is a front for the Diogenes Club. Mycroft's little home away from home. It is one thing to tell us he was expecting a report from Bradstreet, quite another matter entirely not to make us aware that Bradstreet was not just an informant, but an employee."

"Well, in that case, Mr. Holmes, I think we should pay your brother a little visit. Do you not agree?" Lestrade walked past us and got into the cab. He looked back. "Are you gentlemen coming, or not?" he asked.

Chapter Three

In the cab I asked Holmes, "What do you mean by a front for the Diogenes Club?"

"When the Diogenes needs to do something that may bring them out into the open, not a place they particularly care to be, by the way, they use Imperial Exports. You remember the giant rat of Sumatra?"

I shuddered. "I am not sure I will ever forget it!" My dreams now were as equally haunted by the sight of the blood stained teeth of that huge rodent, as they were by the heat, and the blood, and the screams, of Afghanistan.

"It was Imperial Exports antiquities buyers allegedly looking for valuable Buddhist manuscripts that sent a warning that the Matilda Briggs was bound for England with that infernal rodent on board."

Lestrade, who had been with us on that dreadful night at the East India Docks, looked thoughtful. "This Diogenes Club is an official government organization?"

Holmes shook his head. "No, very far from it. It is in fact a gentleman's club. One that serves this city's more unclubbable men. Those who wish comfortable surroundings, good food, recent periodicals, and no interaction with others. My brother was one of the founders. I have myself found the atmosphere contained within its walls to be soothing to the spirit. However, over the last ten years or so it has become the place where information on things that the government, officially, does not want to know about is sorted and problems quietly dealt with."

"But unofficially the government both want and need to know?"

"Exactly!" Holmes nodded at Lestrade with the approving demeanor of a teacher towards a particularly bright student.

"Mycroft sits at the head of this unofficial secret department," Holmes continued. "...and it is he and a few cronies within the halls of the Palace of Westminster who decide what needs to be investigated, or what information needs to be gathered, based on the movements of other nations."

"So that Britain is never at a disadvantage?" I asked.

Holmes turned the approving look upon me. "Just so. Well done, Watson."

"What then is the problem with Bradstreet?" Lestrade asked. "You got into a right lather over Mrs. Bradstreet's little admission."

"Mycroft inferred that Bradstreet was simply an informant. All manner of men provide my brother with information. Barbers, publicans, even our cabbie, may very well be a source of information, but a man who investigates the information provided is a very different creature indeed. One who is immensely more valuable in the scheme of things than a mere supplier of, one hesitates to say 'gossip,' but that is essentially what is being supplied. Though it is gossip of a singular nature far removed from the usual tattle of society drawing rooms."

"How do you know he was not just an informant?" I asked.

"The clothing, Watson. Bradstreet was going out in disguise. There is a certain utility for an agent to do that, but no earthly reason why an informant would need to do so."

Then Holmes frowned. "Nathaniel Croft shaved off his moustache recently. I wonder why."

"What?" said Lestrade, his tone was one of complete bewilderment at the abrupt change of subject.

"His moustache, Lestrade. Croft's upper lip was a lighter shade than the rest of his face. He has obviously had, until recently, a moustache."

Lestrade and I exchanged puzzled looks, and Holmes lapsed into a brooding silence.

When we arrived at the Diogenes Club we were shown straight into the Stranger's Room, the only place within the establishment where talk is permitted, and where Mycroft Holmes was waiting for us. He gestured to us to take seats.

"You have spoken with the widow?"

"We have and we have learned a few potentially valuable things." said Holmes

"Such as?" Mycroft asked.

"That Jeremiah Bradstreet was the second of your people to die in the last three months under questionable circumstances."

"Michael Croft drowned after falling into the Thames. Whether he fell, jumped, or was pushed is not something easily ascertained." said Mycroft.

Holmes looked at his brother. "I would tend to agree, however one must consider the fact that the deaths of two agents, who worked together, and were related by marriage, must surely be linked. It is highly improbable that the situation could be otherwise."

"Jeremiah Bradstreet and Michael Croft were clerks in a minor governmental capacity."

"They were, I believe, employees of Imperial Exports. I know the Diogenes Club is heavily involved with the company. Six of the members serve on the board of directors."

"Besides which," added Lestrade, "it is highly unusual for government clerks to go around dressed as women. I also find it strange that one of your men should die the same barbarous death as a couple of male whores."

Mycroft lowered himself into his chair. He passed a hand over his face and sighed deeply. All at once I became aware of the weight of affairs that pressed upon the shoulders of Mycroft Holmes.

"Perhaps you could also tell us what Bradstreet and Croft were working on," I said. "And let me have a copy of the post mortem report on Croft. I would like a medical man's opinion."

Mycroft gazed at his brother, eyebrows raised in query.

Holmes smiled briefly. "You really do underestimate Watson, brother, and it is never wise to do so with Inspector Lestrade."

Mycroft nodded. "Very well. I shall send a copy of the post-mortem report over to Baker Street as soon as possible, Dr. Watson. A second opinion on the death would be most welcome. As to the other." He paused. "How much do you gentlemen know of the movement for women's enfranchisement?"

"The right to vote, do you mean?" asked Lestrade.

"Yes."

Lestrade shrugged. "It should have been given years ago, when the right to vote for local council was given."

Holmes nodded. "Lestrade is correct. It is ridiculous that our landlady, Mrs. Hudson, as a householder, can vote for local government, but not for someone to best represent her interests in Westminster."

"Especially," I said, "when her tenants, who are possibly the worst tenants in London, can vote."

Mycroft was silent for a moment, contemplating our comments, then sighed. "Perhaps you are all correct. Certainly things have changed since our father's day. Maybe for the better, maybe not. However, that is a concern for another day." He was silent for another moment. "There is a member of the New Zealand Women's Christian Temperance Union currently visiting London," he said at last. "Some powerful members of the government are concerned that she is here to stir up trouble over enfranchisement."

We waited.

"Jeremiah went disguised to her meetings and rallies to discover what, if anything, was happening."

"Why should a visitor from the colonies disturb the government?" asked Lestrade.

"A bill went up before the New Zealand parliament two years ago to give full voting rights to women. It was only narrowly defeated. Government ministers foresee a future bill succeeding. Can you imagine the fury and the disruption here if

New Zealand women have more rights than their British counterparts?"

"The situation is one that is simply fixed," said Holmes. "Give British women the right to vote."

Mycroft glared at him. "You are not taking this seriously, Sherlock."

"Oh but I am, Mycroft. It is just that my view of the situation is exceedingly different from yours. Come, we need the lady's name and where she can be found."

"You plan to interview her? I am not sure that that can be permitted. It could jeopardize the entire undertaking."

"It seems to me," said Lestrade, "that your undertaking was destroyed with the deaths of Bradstreet and Croft. Nothing is to be lost now by visiting the lady."

Mycroft thought about this for a moment, before conceding the point. "You may very well be correct, Inspector. The lady is Mrs. May Cunningham. A widow of private means. She is staying at the Northumberland Hotel."

"Excellent." Holmes rubbed his hands together. "We shall visit her in the morning. It is getting a little late in the evening to be disturbing honest women." He looked across at Lestrade. "You will meet us at the Northumberland Hotel at 10 o'clock?"

"Of course, Mr. Holmes."

"Excellent. Come Watson, if we are fortunate Mrs. Hudson will have held supper for us."

The next morning found us, along with Lestrade, ensconced in the front parlour of the Northumberland Hotel with Mrs. May Cunningham. The lady in question was a widow of about forty years of age, short, matronly, with a round, open face, shrewd blue eyes, and mouse-brown hair that was slowly fading to gray.

She poured the tea that the hotel's manager had provided for us, then sat back and observed us over the rim of her cup. "Tell me, what can I do for the famous Sherlock Holmes, the equally famous Doctor Watson, and Inspector Lestrade of Scotland Yard?"

"We just have a few questions for you, ma'am," said Lestrade.

"Questions? How intriguing." Mrs. Cunningham sipped her tea and waited. She reminded me of a cat sitting patiently outside a mouse hole.

"You have held a few quite meetings and rallies since you arrived four months ago," Holmes said. "Have you noticed anything unusual at these events?"

"Apart from the man dressed as a woman, or including him?" she asked.

We all stared at her.

She chuckled softly. "He really did stand out, you know. Did it not occur to him to cover his throat with either a velvet choker or a high collar? The prominent Adam's apple was somewhat obvious."

"Obvious to you, ma'am," said Holmes. "but, alas, not everyone is as observant as you are. Most people would see the dress and see a woman."

"Very true. And also very wrong." Mrs. Cunningham placed her cup and saucer upon the table and sat back, hands folded in her lap. "This is why we want enfranchisement. Women should have the right to be seen as individual people, not simply representatives of their sex." The look she gave us was challenging. We all nodded in agreement.

"Did the man do anything unusual?" Lestrade asked.

Mrs. Cunningham seemed vaguely disappointed that we were not prepared to argue with her.

"He took notes," she said. "That is not common, but not unusual. To be honest, I thought he was a reporter. You know what they are like."

"Indeed," said Holmes. "Mrs. Cunningham, I admit that I am intrigued by your visit. It is somewhat remarkable for someone to visit from the colonies to hold meetings. Usually someone goes from here to disseminate the latest political ideas."

"That is very true, Mr. Holmes. Except that, in this instance, the colony of New Zealand is far ahead of the motherland. You are aware of our history towards enfranchisement?"

"Yes. I believe the last bill placed before your parliament was only narrowly defeated."

I could hear the echo of Mycroft's tone in his words.

"It is very likely that within the next five years we shall see enfranchisement for the women of New Zealand. There are people here who wish Britain's women to know what is happening. Sir Lucas Catterick invited Katherine Sheppard to visit. He is an avid supporter of women's rights. Brought up by his mother and grandmother, I understand. Both of them strong women with modern attitudes."

Mrs. Cunningham stopped, picked up her cup and saucer, and took another sip of her tea. "Poor Kate is unwell though, and was unable to accept his kind invitation, so the Women's Christian Temperance Union sent me instead. I have as much fire as Kate, though possibly a little more tact."

I hid a smile. Mrs. May Cunningham was about as tactful as Holmes on one of his bad days. I saw Lestrade concealing a smile as well.

Holmes smiled graciously and rose to his feet. "Thank you for your time, Mrs. Cunningham. I wish you every success with your endeavor." Lestrade and I rose as well, said goodbye, and followed Holmes out of the hotel.

Outside, as we hailed a cab, Lestrade said, "Well that was a wasted visit."

"Nonsense, Lestrade. We have several new pieces of information."

"Oh?"

"Watson?" Holmes turned to me. "Enlighten Lestrade."

I was surprised at Holmes' turning to me. "Well, we do know that Bradstreet attended the meetings disguised as a woman," I said, dragged out of my thoughts by Holmes' comment.

"Badly disguised," said Holmes. "What else…?"

"We have a new name. Sir Lucas Catterick."

"Excellent. Sir Lucas Catterick. Fifth baronet Undershaw, from memory."

"What has he to do with anything, Mr. Holmes?" asked Lestrade.

"We do not know yet, Inspector. Maybe nothing, maybe everything. Time alone will tell."

Lestrade returned to Scotland Yard, and we returned to Baker Street.

Mycroft Holmes was waiting in our rooms, seated in the guest chair. I was surprised to see him. His presence in our rooms was an indication of how concerned he was about the situation. As I have previously written, Mycroft Holmes was man of circular and regular habits. He went from his lodgings, to his office in Whitehall, to the Diogenes Club and back to his rooms. It was extremely rare for him to break the pattern, and he had done so twice in two days.

Mycroft gestured to a folder of papers waiting on the desk. "The post-mortem report on Michael Croft."

I hurried across and picked it up, seated myself in my chair, and tried to ignore the Holmes brothers, which was not an easy task at the best of times.

"Did you learn anything interesting, Sherlock?" asked Mycroft.

"Only that Jeremiah Bradstreet did not make a very adept spy. The lady spotted him quite early on. Have you considered employing female agents, Mycroft? They do seem to be more observant than your men. Mrs. Bradstreet found her husband's disguise, and Mrs. Cunningham saw straight through it."

"Preposterous! The very idea!"

I looked up briefly to catch a glimpse of Mycroft Holmes' swiftly concealed expression of outrage.

"The idea is a very sound one," said Holmes. "It just is not one that you are prepared to entertain. The Pinkerton Agency, for example, has female agents."

"That is America, Sherlock. This is Britain. We do things differently here."

I skimmed through the post-mortem report. It was quite obvious that Michael Croft had drowned; all the signs were there. Then I found a note from the examining doctor.

"Good Lord!" I said, my voice heavy with shock.

"What is it, Watson?" asked Holmes.

He turned away from his brother to turn curious eyes upon me.

Frowning slightly, I looked at Mycroft. "Was Michael Croft married?"

Mycroft shook his head. "No. He was of the opinion that his job left him no time to contemplate marriage. Indeed, he often remarked that he considered himself to be wedded to his work. A pretty conceit, I will admit."

I could not restrain a cynical snort. Both Holmes brothers raised their eyebrows at me.

"He was remarkably unfaithful," I said, with some asperity.

"What do you mean?" asked Holmes.

I read from the report. "I note in passing that the deceased had the beginnings of syphilitic chancres or sores forming around the genital area."

"Interesting," observed Holmes.

"But not necessarily useful," said Mycroft.

"It is still far too early to say what information will eventually prove to be of use. I shall file this away, along with the obvious fact that Michael Croft was a liar, until I have some puzzle pieces that actually fit together."

Mycroft looked troubled. "I do not like to think that Croft was not trustworthy."

"He was most likely ashamed," I said. "That does not make him untrustworthy."

"Perhaps not," said Mycroft. He inclined his head to me and to Holmes. "Good day, Sherlock, Dr. Watson. Do let me know when you have something substantive." He walked out of our rooms.

I rose from my seat, went to stand at the window, and watched Mycroft flag down a cab, no doubt heading back to Whitehall.

Holmes came across and took the report from me, turned away, and began to read it for himself. "Hmmm. All fairly straightforward. Water from the Thames in the lungs. Ante-mortem and post-mortem injuries from being bounced about in the river. Including multiple bone fractures. Body found near St. Katherine's Docks. Speculation that he went into the water near Westminster Bridge. How did they...? Ahhhh. Based on tidal patterns. Hmmm. Only thing of interest, as you have noticed, is the reference to syphilis."

Holmes put the report down on the desk, walked to the window, and stood beside me. He stood there, staring down at Baker Street, and brooding.

I cast around for something to discuss about the case that would stop him sinking further into a dark mood. I moved away from the window and returned to my chair at the desk.

"Do you think Sir Lucas Catterick may be involved in all this somehow?" I asked, as I sat down.

"I do not know, Watson, but we may have the chance to find out."

"What do you mean?" I asked.

"A fine carriage has just drawn up outside our door. Very modern. The sort of thing one expects to belong to a rich baronet."

I rose from my seat and hurried to stand beside Holmes, looking down into the street. A handsome, red-headed, man alighted from the carriage, strode lightly up the steps, and rang the bell. Shortly afterwards, Mrs. Hudson showed him into our rooms.

The man would have been in his early thirties, with the pale complexion usually associated with red hair. He looked from Holmes to me and back again, green eyes dancing in enquiry. "Mr. Sherlock Holmes? Dr. John Watson?" His voice held the faint traces of a Scottish accent.

Holmes waved a hand. "I am Sherlock Holmes, and this is my friend and colleague, John Watson. Do sit down, sir, and tell us what has brought you here to Baker Street."

"Thank you, Mr. Holmes, I shall not sit," the man said. "I am Thomas Arbuthnot, secretary to Sir Lucas Catterick." He took an envelope from his inside coat pocket, and handed it to Holmes. "Sir Lucas asked me to give you this, and request that you join him for tea this afternoon."

Holmes opened the envelope and glanced at the message. "Please convey our regards to Sir Lucas, and tell him that we will be happy to attend him at his Kensington house."

Arbuthnot nodded, turned, and went down the stairs.

I waited until I heard the street door close, then turned to Holmes. "Should we advise Lestrade?"

"I do not think so." Holmes turned the letter towards me so I could read it. "The letter clearly states "Mr. Sherlock Holmes and Dr. John Watson". Lestrade has not been invited. It is extremely bad manners to turn up with an uninvited guest."

"Since when has displaying bad manners worried you?"

"On this occasion, Watson, I do believe prudence is called for."

Chapter Four

The cab dropped us in front of a charming townhouse. Modern and attractive, it radiated quiet good taste. A butler answered our knock. Behind him, a young maidservant passed hurriedly through the hall, a small pile of linens in her arms.

"Mr. Sherlock Holmes and Dr. John Watson to see Sir Lucas," my friend said.

The butler bowed slightly. "This way, please, gentlemen, Sir Lucas is expecting you."

We were shown into a bright, sunny parlour, scented with vases of spring flowers. Thomas Arbuthnot was waiting for us. "Please take a seat, gentlemen. Sir Lucas will be joining us shortly."

Before I could sit down, the butler returned. "Excuse me, Dr. Watson. Lady Caroline has heard that you are here, and wishes to speak with you."

I looked at Arbuthnot, raising my eyebrows slightly in enquiry.

Arbuthnot smiled slightly. "Lady Caroline is Sir Lucas' grandmother. She is currently bedridden. The maid who looks after her must have heard Mr. Holmes introducing yourselves."

I looked up at the butler. "I do not have my bag with me, but I am happy to speak with Lady Caroline if she wishes."

The butler inclined his head and left the room, with me hurrying after him. I was led up an elegant flight of stairs to a stately, but still rather comfortable, bedroom with wide windows that overlooked a garden. The scent coming through the open windows suggested the source of the flowers so prominently displayed in the parlour.

A large bed contained a rather formidable looking, though somewhat frail, elderly lady whom one could describe as a grand dame without fear of contradiction. She looked at me with bright, intelligent, blue eyes. A lock of silver hair escaped from beneath the lawn nightcap she wore.

"Good afternoon, Lady Caroline. I am Doctor John Watson. I am told that you wish to see me?"

She beckoned me towards the bed. I reached out to take hold of her wrist to take her pulse, when her hand closed firmly around my wrist, and she dragged me closer. Lady Caroline obviously was not quite as frail as she appeared.

"Leave my grandson alone." Her voice was firm and steady.

"I beg your pardon?"

"I know why you are here."

"That is far more than I do, ma'am."

"Do not be facetious with me, young man. You and that other jackanapes are here to take my grandson away. Someone has told you that he is different."

I could see anxiety and fear in her eyes, though she tried to hide it. I may not be the most intelligent of men. Certainly not as intelligent as my friend Sherlock Holmes, but I thought of his earlier comments about learning to see beyond the surface appearances, and quickly linked the lady's fear, with the letter from Sir Lucas, and the case.

I gently unclasped her hand from my wrist.

"Please calm yourself, Lady Caroline. I assure you, you have nothing to fear. Sir Lucas himself invited us here. I think that whoever told you I am a doctor missed the name of my companion, leading you to an erroneous conclusion. My companion is Sherlock Holmes."

Lady Caroline eyed me narrowly. "The detective?"

That was good. She knew the name. I nodded. "The very same."

Lady Caroline continued to scrutinize me closely. "You do not look much like the illustrations in the Strand magazine," she said.

"The artist exercises a little license in that respect," I said.

"You are much handsomer than the pictures give you credit for."

I felt my ears turning red. Lady Caroline laughed and clapped her hands with glee. "Please forgive me, Dr. Watson, at my age one of the few pleasures left to me is embarrassing the young."

Her eyes twinkled with mischief, and, I noted, more than a little relief.

"Nothing to forgive, Lady Caroline," I said.

"Mother?"

I looked towards the doorway. A tall lady, dark hair lightly touched with silver at the temples, stood there, the butler standing respectfully behind her. She hurried into the room.

"I am sorry, Dr. Watson. Jenkins told me you had been asked up here. Mother did not know that Luce invited you."

"That is quite all right," I said.

"This is my daughter, Amelia," Lady Caroline said. "Lady Amelia Catterick. Luce's mother."

I bowed slightly. "A pleasure to meet you, Lady Amelia. I assure you, visiting your mother was no hardship. I was able to set her mind at rest."

"I am so pleased," said Lady Amelia. "Jenkins will escort you back downstairs to your meeting."

I bowed again, this time to both ladies, and followed the butler from the room.

May Cunningham had been correct in her assumptions. Sir Lucas Catterick's mother and grandmother were, indeed, strong women.

A man of middling height had joined my friend and Arbuthnot in the parlour. He was willow slender with blonde hair and china blue eyes that reminded me of Lady Caroline. A wide, welcoming smile swept across his face when he saw me. "Welcome, Dr. Watson, I am sorry if my grandmother inconvenienced you."

"Not at all, Sir Lucas. Lady Caroline is a charming, if somewhat formidable, woman," I said.

The smile grew wider. "She is indeed. Please, have a seat while we wait for tea, and then I will explain why I invited you and Mr. Holmes here."

I looked at Holmes with raised eyebrows. His expression was slightly sour. "Sir Lucas insisted on waiting until you joined us," he said.

I hid a smile. There were few things that Holmes liked less than making small talk. To have been forced to do so with

Sir Lucas and Thomas Arbuthnot would have been purgatory for him.

We waited until the butler and a maid brought in a fine china teapot, cups, and an excellent selection of sandwiches, scones with jam and cream, and cake. It was all I could do not to lick my lips. Mrs. Hudson could not have served a finer spread.

Sir Lucas served us all with tea and handed around the plates of comestibles. I bit into a fine roast beef sandwich, and settled back to listen to what Sir Lucas had to tell us.

Holmes merely sipped politely at his tea before returning the cup to its saucer, and turning towards our host. "The pleasantries have been observed. Now, Sir Lucas, why have we been summoned here?" he asked bluntly.

I winced, carefully setting down my cup and saucer. "Please excuse my friend, patience is not his strongest virtue. Neither are good manners." Holmes glared at me. I ignored him in favour of taking another bite of my sandwich.

A look of amusement passed between Sir Lucas and Thomas Arbuthnot. "It is not a problem, Dr. Watson. Mr. Holmes' foibles are well known," said Sir Lucas. "However, Mr. Holmes is right to be impatient. There are things that he needs to know, if only to stop the wrong people being persecuted."

Holmes turned to our host with an expression of intense curiosity on his face.

Sir Lucas looked uncomfortable. "It is hard to know where to start, gentlemen. In giving you the information you need, I am placing my secret into your hands."

Thomas Arbuthnot laid a gentle hand on the baronet's shoulder. I heard him murmur "I am sure Mr. Holmes and Dr. Watson can be trusted, Luce."

Holmes held up a hand. "I have already deduced your secret, Sir Lucas," he said softly. "When we shook hands, your hands were softer than those of other men, even those that do not do manual labour. I felt upon your hand the residue from a cream such as ladies use to soften their skin, and keep their hands blemish free. When you move it is with an almost unconscious sway of the hips, as though used to wearing corsets on a regular basis. Then there is the faint scent of violets that lingers around you. An unusual scent to find on a man."

Holmes gave Sir Lucas a look filled with compassion. "The unavoidable conclusion is that you are, Sir Lucas, what some members of the medical profession call, a He/She Lady."

Sir Lucas gaped open-mouthed at my friend. "That is incredible."

Holmes shrugged. "A mere trifle of observation."

Sir Lucas floundered, trying to gather his thoughts.

"It also goes without saying," I said, "that anything you tell us will be held in the strictest confidence. You will not wake up one morning and find this case in Strand Magazine. On that you have my sworn word."

Sir Lucas gave us both a grateful look. "Thank you gentlemen. You can understand why I did not invite Inspector Lestrade to join us."

Holmes smiled briefly. "Inside the façade of a Scotland Yard dullard that Lestrade wears, there beats the heart of a compassionate man. Already noises are being made in the upper levels of the Yard about wasting money on tracking the killer of deviants. Lestrade is making noises back at them. He is a great believer in justice for everyone, regardless of what the upper echelon thinks. Which is why he will never rise above Inspector, and that will be a great loss for London."

"Why Holmes," I said. "I never realized you thought so highly of Lestrade."

Holmes looked sideways at me. "He has no need to know my opinion. The man would just strut more like a bantam cock than ever."

"Well, as you gentleman now know my secret, we had best move on to other matters," said Sir Lucas.

Holmes and I returned our attention to our host.

"You have, along with Inspector Lestrade, been to talk with both May Cunningham and Gertrude Swindon. I would be interested to know how the two connect in your mind before I tell you a few things. If you do not mind confiding in me."

"There may not be a connection at all, Sir Lucas," said Holmes. "It is just there is a rather unusual link from Mrs. Cunningham to the killings. Whether there is a further link from Mrs. Cunningham to Mrs. Swindon is still a matter of mere conjecture."

"Oh?"

"A quasi-government agent was investigating Mrs. Cunningham's ventures here. He was found murdered in the same manner as the two young whores."

Sir Lucas frowned. "Am I correct in assuming that this agent is the man dressed as a woman that May thought was a reporter?"

"Indeed," said Holmes.

"And the government has been investigating May, you say?"

"The idea that women are equal to men, and deserve equal rights, makes certain high-placed men very nervous," I said.

"That is ridiculous," said Arbuthnot, with a derisive sniff. "Our monarch is a woman. That makes her greater than any man in the Empire."

"I do not believe that such a thought has occurred to any of these men, Mr. Arbuthnot," said Holmes. "Intelligence not being a prerequisite in a politician."

"Unfortunate, but true," said Sir Lucas. "May Cunningham's visit is, in part, being financed by myself. I support a number of female emancipation societies."

"Your reasoning being that if women have equal rights with men, then it will be but a short step to people such as yourself being generally accepted?" asked Holmes.

"I realize that it is a long bow to draw, Mr. Holmes, but we must start somewhere. People like myself will never gain acceptance, or even much in the way of understanding, if woman are still being treated as second-class citizens."

"Pray forgive me, Sir Lucas," said Holmes, "but do you truly think that politicians will give, what many view as sexual deviants, as much as a passing thought, let alone recognize them as equals?"

Sir Lucas sighed. "Those such as myself live tentative lives on the very edge of society, Mr. Holmes. We are always fearful of discovery, of ostracism, of persecution, or worse. No human being should have to spend his life in fear."

Holmes nodded his agreement. "I understand, Sir Lucas."

"You mentioned Gertrude Swindon," I said.

"Gertrude is a cousin of mine," said Sir Lucas.

I stared at him open-mouthed. Sir Lucas was related to a bawd?

"We grew up together. Gertrude is well aware of what I am, and understands. That is why we run the house."

"We?" asked Holmes.

"I own the house in Cleveland Street, Mr. Holmes. Gertrude ostensibly rents the house from me. She and I keep an eye out for young men like myself. Many are, unfortunately, selling themselves on the streets when we find them. We take them in and try to turn their lives around. Let them understand that they are not alone. We train them to be teachers, or type-writers, or help them set up business in a shop. Most of them end up on the Continent, or in America, living lives of quiet, respectable, unmarried women, which is really all the majority of them want. We give them new identities and new pasts. Mostly as widows. People tend to understand if a widow does not wish to marry again. They get to live their lives as their true selves, not what society thinks they should be."

"And the minority?" asked Holmes.

Sir Lucas' face was a study in unhappiness. "There are some who still go back to the streets. Those we try to keep as safe as we can, without compromising ourselves."

"Which is why David Clutterbuck, also known as Molly, was still living in Cleveland Street," said Holmes.

Sir Lucas nodded. My friend got to his feet and I followed. Sir Lucas rose as well to show us out.

In the doorway my friend paused. "One more thing, Sir Lucas, if I am not being too personal, how do you reconcile who you perceive yourself to be, with your duty to provide an heir?"

Sir Lucas smiled faintly. "I have a brother, Mr. Holmes, and two nephews. The title is in safe hands."

We shook hands with Sir Lucas and Thomas Arbuthnot and turned to leave. Jenkins held the door open for us.

From behind me I heard a voice call my name.

I turned to see Lady Amelia coming down the stairs. She laid a hand on my arm. "I have a favour to ask of you, Doctor."

"Anything, Lady Amelia," I said.

"My mother was rather taken with you, Doctor Watson. She wonders if you might call upon her and regale her with some stories from yours and Mr. Holmes' investigations. It is very boring for her, trapped in that room all day, and she has, alas, outlived most of her friends."

I made a formal little bow. "Lady Amelia, please tell Lady Caroline that I will be happy to call on her. I will send word before I come."

Lady Amelia beamed at me. "Thank you, Doctor Watson, it will be very much appreciated." She hurried back up the stairs.

Sir Lucas laughed. "You must really have made an impression, Doctor Watson. My grandmother rarely takes to anyone new." His eyes twinkled. "My grandmother dislikes doctors on general principle, but she does eagerly await each issue of Strand Magazine."

"I will be only too happy to help alleviate her boredom, once this case is finished," I said.

"Thank you."

We took our leave and hastened out into the street to hail a cab. Settled in comfortably, Holmes looked at me. "What happened with Lady Caroline?" he asked.

I sighed. "She feared we were there to take her grandson to a lunatic asylum."

Holmes nodded. "I surmised as much. The maid in the hallway looked rather furtive when she heard the word 'doctor.' Men such as Sir Lucas lead such tentative lives."

"They do."

Silence fell as the cab rumbled on its way back to Baker Street.

Chapter Five

Holmes waited until we had returned to our rooms to properly broach the subject of Sir Lucas Catterick. He filled his pipe with tobacco from his tattered, old Persian slipper, then settled down into his chair to puff meditatively for a few minutes before speaking.

I relaxed in my chair and waited for him to break the silence.

"Well, Watson, what did you make of Sir Lucas?"

I marshalled my thoughts carefully. "I think he is an unfortunate individual. I cannot imagine living my life feeling that I were someone other than what I was physically born as. Such people are much more common than we think. There was a soldier I tended who was injured just before I was." I rubbed my shoulder reflectively. "A brave young man. Always the first in to a battle and the last out. Eventually his luck ran out and he caught a bullet. Luckily for him it merely scrapped the surface of the skin and failed to penetrate. He was brought to me in a haze of pain and blood. Upon removing his tunic I discovered something interesting."

Holmes waited patiently for me to finish, no doubt wondering what my reminiscences had to do with Sir Lucas.

I gazed into the fire place. I could feel Holmes' eyes on me. I looked up at him. "I found that he was in fact a she."

Holmes voice was soft. "What did you do?"

"Dressed the wound, got him a fresh tunic, and recommended a promotion to officer. Less chance of his secret being discovered that way."

"Watson, I swear that I never get your measure."

"It is really not that uncommon, Holmes. Many women have gone to war as soldiers. Most are not discovered until they are killed in battle. If there are women who feel that they are men, then why should there not be men who feel that they are truly women?"

"A valid point, my friend. And we have met two such individuals within a very short space of time. Sir Lucas today, and young Daniel at Mrs. Swindon's establishment. Though as a courtesy I suppose we should find out which name he prefers. It seems a trifle impolite to use Daniel when he clearly is not a Daniel."

"Danielle, perhaps?"

Holmes shrugged. "Possibly. Or something far removed, as Molly Clutterbuck's name was. I wonder what name Sir Lucas prefers."

"His mother, grandmother, and young Arbuthnot all called him Luce. That is a diminutive for Lucas, but also for Lucille or Lucinda." I had been wondering that myself since Sir Lucas' secret had been revealed by Holmes.

"A good point, Watson. Perhaps we shall know one day. In any case, it has no bearing on the work before us."

I nodded. A thought struck me. "Holmes, what are we going to tell Lestrade?"

Holmes cocked his head to one side and studied me for a few moments. "What do you think we should tell him?"

"He really should know about Gertrude Swindon," I said.

"Agreed."

"But…" I hesitated.

"What is it, Watson?"

"Is it the right thing to tell him about Sir Lucas?"

Holmes looked thoughtful. "No, Watson, I do not believe that it is. It is one thing to give him a relatively harmless piece of information. Almost our duty to, if only to stop him making a fool of himself over Mrs. Swindon. But to give him another man's secret, and one that could potentially open Sir Lucas to serious allegations, if not felony charges, no, I do not think we have a right to do that."

"Serious allegations? Felony charges?" I was momentarily bewildered.

"Come, Watson, you saw Thomas Arbuthnot."

I thought for a moment about the young man's gentle solicitousness towards Sir Lucas and the penny dropped. "Ah! You mean charges of unnatural conduct."

"Exactly. Let us not expose those two to more dangers than they already face in their lives."

I nodded my agreement. "So, we are agreed then, we only tell Lestrade about Gertrude Swindon."

"Yes. Send him an invitation to supper, if you please, Watson. This need not be formal. Besides, living alone in his room in Westminster, and existing on meat pies from street vendors is not good for him."

I was not going to give Holmes the satisfaction of asking how he knew of Lestrade's domestic arrangements, but the thought must have shown on my face.

Holmes smiled briefly. "Wiggins, and myself, have both spotted him going into a lodging house not far from Scotland Yard on several occasions. It is one that a number of single police officers chose to dwell in. As for the meat pies. I have seen the flakes of pastry upon his coat lapels on numerous occasions."

I got up from my chair and turned to go down the stairs to send the telegram.

"Oh, and Watson? Please ask Mrs. Hudson to throw a few more sausages in the pan for tonight's supper."

Even I knew how he had deduced sausages for supper. I had seen the butcher's boy delivering the links that very morning.

When I returned upstairs, Holmes was now standing by the window, gazing out into the street below. He turned to look at me as I entered.

"The telegram has been sent."

Holmes nodded, then he threw himself into his armchair and reached once more for the Persian slipper. "Then there is nothing more to be said until Lestrade arrives."

I nodded, took my accustomed chair, and picked up that afternoon's newspaper.

Lestrade arrived shortly after 7 o'clock. I went down to let him in, as Mrs. Hudson was busy in the kitchen. He sniffed appreciatively at the delicious smells coming from that room, and smiled at me. "It is very kind of you to invite me to supper, Dr. Watson."

"Pray do not mention it, Inspector. We came into some information this afternoon. Nothing urgent, so it seemed best to pass it on informally."

I kept to myself the surmise that when he found out that Gertrude Swindon was not what he thought she was, Lestrade would be damn near apoplectic. Having him here in a more domestic setting made him less likely to get too angry.

Holmes turned a slight smile on Lestrade as we entered our rooms. "Lestrade. Come in. Sit down." He gestured to the table that was laid for three. "Mrs. Hudson will be bringing supper up shortly. Talk can wait until after we have eaten. Some things are best discussed on a full stomach."

Mrs. Hudson arrived just then with the food, and we tucked into plates of sausages with onion gravy, potatoes, and green beans. A good, hearty, meal. All that was heard for a while were requests to pass the salt, the bread, and the butter. Finally, Lestrade sat back and dabbed at his lips and moustache with his napkin.

Mrs. Hudson came to clear the plates. Lestrade smiled at her. "Thank you for as fine a meal as I have eaten in a long while. You are a queen of the kitchen, ma'am."

I may have given the impression in my earlier writings that our landlady was elderly. This was far from the truth. Mrs. Hudson was a fine, matronly, woman of around thirty five, with dark hair with a hint a chestnut threaded through it, and warm, brown eyes like a mischievous doe. Her husband had been killed by a hansom cab when crossing the road, leaving her a youngish widow of property, and with no inclination to sample the married state again.

To my amazement, Mrs. Hudson blushed. "Away with you and your flattery, Inspector." She patted him lightly on the shoulder.

"Watson."

"Yes, Holmes?"

"I do believe that the good inspector is flirting with our landlady."

"It certainly looks like it, Holmes."

Laughing to herself, Mrs. Hudson carried the plates out of the room. Lestrade turned a fake scowl on us both. Then he laughed somewhat ruefully. "If it were not for the fact you invited me to this excellent meal, I would tell you both exactly what I thought."

Holmes waved a hand airily. "Do not let that stop you, Lestrade. I am always keen to hear your opinions. You know what great value I place upon them."

Smiling, I got up to pour brandy for us all.

Holmes and Lestrade moved from the table to the armchairs. Lestrade settled back comfortably, took a sip of his brandy, and waited for Holmes to speak.

"Since we last spoke, Watson and I have learned one or two things that may be related to the case. The first one relates to Gertrude Swindon. To be blunt about it the lady is not a bawd."

Lestrade spluttered brandy. "What?"

"The young men who live with her are not exactly young men," I said.

"They look like men, Doctor," said Lestrade. "Talk like men. Walk like men."

"But they do not think or feel like men," I said.

Lestrade gave me a hard look. "You mean they are he/she ladies?"

"Yes," said Holmes. "Mrs. Swindon is not pimping them. That good lady is trying to get them safely to somewhere where they can live quiet lives as the women they know themselves to be. Some of them come from the street, and frequently return to it, despite Mrs. Swindon's best efforts."

Lestrade was silent for a while. "Gets them somewhere else, you said?"

"To the Continent," said Holmes. "Or to America, where they lead the lives of unmarried women, mostly posing as young widows."

"That would cost a lot of money," said Lestrade. "Someone must be financing it."

"That would be her cousin, Sir Lucas Catterick," said Holmes.

"That makes sense." Lestrade took a meditative sip of brandy. "Sir Lucas being a he/she lady as well."

I blinked in surprise.

Holmes raised his eyebrows, a look of quiet surprise on his face. "Sometimes, Lestrade, you amaze me quite as much as Watson does."

"Thank you. I think," said Lestrade, his expression wry.

"How do you know Sir Lucas' secret?" I asked.

Lestrade shrugged. "I saw him at the court with that secretary chap when Gertrude Swindon was before the Beak. I have met a few of his like before, mostly on the streets. It was fairly obvious what he was, when you know the signs."

"Yet you never made a fuss," I said.

"Why should I?" Lestrade asked. "He is not breaking any law, so far as I can tell. What people do and feel and think is none of my business, unless it breaks the laws of Great Britain. And feeling and thinking were not a crime the last time I looked. Of course, with the way this government is going, who can tell what is going to be a criminal activity come next week?"

Lestrade took another sip of his brandy. "I suppose that's why he is supporting Mrs. Cunningham's endeavours as well. Freedom for women could easily become freedom for all."

Holmes took a sip from his own glass. "That is two surprises in one evening, Lestrade", he observed drily.

Lestrade laughed, and set his glass down on the table. "Thank you for the supper and the conversation, gentleman. It is time I was leaving. You will let me know if you obtain any information that actually helps the case?"

"Of course," said Holmes.

Lestrade got up and headed for the door.

We remained seated, quietly drinking our brandy as Lestrade's footsteps retreated and we heard the street door open and close.

Chapter Six

Breakfast had been cleared away next morning, and Holmes and I were ensconced in our arm chairs with the morning papers, when Mrs. Hudson showed in a visitor.

I looked up with some surprise into the sheepish face of Nathaniel Croft.

He looked from myself to Holmes and back again. "I have come to apologize for my behaviour the other day, gentlemen. I have been unable to deal with Michael's death. I had been drinking since quite early that morning, and my behaviour was most certainly not that of a gentleman." His voice was virtually expressionless. He sounded to me like a schoolboy who had learned a little speech by rote and was trotting it out for his teachers.

Holmes looked at him for a long moment, then rose from his seat. "Think nothing of it, Mr. Croft. These are trying times for you and for your sister." Holmes' tone was cool.

"You are very kind, Mr. Holmes. Once again, my apologies." Croft sketched a little bow to us both and took his leave.

Holmes sat back down.

"What do you make of that?" I asked.

"Poppycock, my dear Watson. Pure, unrefined, poppycock."

"Would you care to explain, Holmes?"

"Croft's excuse for his behaviour that morning is that he was drunk."

"Correct."

"He was not."

"How do you know?"

"When we arrived and he entered the hall behaving in a belligerent fashion whilst you were tending to Mrs. Bradstreet, you remember that Lestrade shoved him up against the wall?"

"That part is a little hard to forget. You and Lestrade confronting him whilst I removed his sister to the parlour."

"The man is a liar. He was breathing in my face Watson. There was no smell of alcohol on his breath. Yet when he came back when we were all in the parlour he smelled strongly of whiskey."

I frowned in thought. "We were not in there much more than 30 minutes, if indeed that long. There is no way he could have got so comprehensively drunk in such a short period of time."

"Exactly, Watson. I knew something was not right at the time, but I could not quite identify what it was. I realized it just now whilst Croft was speaking."

"Then why pretend to be drunk? Why come and apologize now?"

"As to the first, I have no notion, but I am filing the information away in case it proves useful to the matter at hand. Any aberrent behaviour may prove to be relevant. In regards to the second, I suspect that Mrs. Bradstreet has had more than a few words to say to her brother on the subject of his behaviour."

"Mrs. Bradstreet certainly struck me as a lady who would brook no nonsense." I said.

"We are surrounded by strong-minded women in this case, Watson."

"We are indeed, Holmes."

"Refreshing, is it not?"

I laughed and reached for my discarded newspaper. "Oh yes. It certainly makes for a vast change from damsels in distress."

Holmes picked up his own newspaper, and silence returned to our rooms. We sat that way for around half an hour before Holmes tossed his paper to one side. I looked across at him, eyebrows raised.

"I cannot just sit here doing nothing, Watson," he said.

"What can we do, Holmes? We have no lines of enquiry to follow at the moment."

"I think we need to talk further with Mrs. Bradstreet. Nathaniel Croft's odd behaviour is pricking at me. A further talk with the lady may prove to be beneficial to the case."

"Then let us, by all means, return to Putney."

"You have nothing you need to be doing today?"

"Nothing that cannot be put aside. Like yourself, I am concerned that we have not been able to get a viable lead on the killer. Even if Mrs. Bradstreet has nothing useful to tell us, at least we will feel as if we are doing something."

"Perhaps you should retrain as an alienist, my friend. You are beginning to sound like one." Holmes was all high good humour once again.

I laughed. "Perhaps you could consider it as a part-time occupation yourself, aside from detecting. The two appear to have much in common in the seeking out of clues to human behaviour."

I folded my newspaper and placed it aside, then we donned our coats and left Baker Street.

As we exited the cab outside the Bradstreet house, the door was opened for us by Mary, who must have seen the cab arrive. She bobbed a little curtsey, and escorted us into the parlour before going to fetch Mrs. Bradstreet.

Viola Bradstreet joined us shortly afterwards. Holmes rose to his feet. "Good morning, Mrs. Bradstreet. We are sorry to intrude once again upon your mourning, but we felt we should call and see how you are coping, and if you have perchance remembered or encountered anything that may help us in tracking the killer."

Mrs. Bradstreet sat carefully upon the small sofa, arranging her skirts around her. She looked thoughtful. "What sort of things do you mean, Mr. Holmes?"

"It has been my experience that the strangest of things may have relevance to a case. Anything out of place, no matter how small, may prove to be crucial, even if we do not realize it at the time. Many a case has been solved by a small oddity that did not appear to be of importance as the time."

There was silence as Mary wheeled in a tea trolley and served us with excellent China tea, and laid out a selection of small cakes and sandwiches. Having had breakfast not that long ago, I merely took a small cake for politeness sake, and sipped my tea. It was very good tea.

Mrs. Bradstreet tasted her tea, a small frown forming between her eyes. "There was a man at the funeral who behaved rather oddly."

My friend leaned forward avidly. "That could be useful. What did this man look like? How did he act?"

"He was an extremely fat man. Rather tall and with sharp grey eyes. He said nothing at all before or after the service, just gave me ten pounds and left. I found that rather worrying. I have hidden the money away in case it turned out to be stolen."

Holmes leaned back in his seat and smiled gently. "You do not need to worry on that account, ma'am. I know who that man was."

"Mycroft?" I asked.

"Just so." Holmes turned back to Mrs. Bradstreet, "The man was the employer of your husband and brother. You may view the money as being a slight compensation for your loss."

"He had an odd way to him."

"The gentleman in question does not really know how to deal with women, Mrs. Bradstreet. He lives his life completely surrounded by men. He means well, however."

"That is indeed reassuring, Mr. Holmes." Mrs. Bradstreet took another sip of her tea. "I really cannot think of anything else."

Mary, who was refilling our teacups murmured in her mistress' ear. "What about the dress, ma'am?"

"Oh good heavens! You are correct, Mary, that is very odd."

Holmes raised an eyebrow in query.

"Just before you arrived with news of Jeremiah's death, Mary and I had been sorting my wardrobe to prepare for my coming out of mourning for Michael. We discovered that there was a dress missing. It is one I had laid aside because it was designed for a much larger bustle than those currently in fashion. I had intended to reshape it for a smaller bustle, but had not had a chance to do so before Michael's death. It had been packed in a trunk in the attic, along with my other clothing. When we were sorting the clothing, we discovered one trunk had been opened and ruffled through. The only thing missing was the dress. I was really quite cross about it, as that dress was one of my favourites. A very pretty spring green damask silk, with gold lace at cuffs and neck, and gold buttons."

Holmes looked at me pointedly. "Kindly make a note of that, if you please, Watson."

I hurriedly got out my notebook and jotted down the description of the dress. Why Holmes thought this could be important, was beyond my comprehension.

"Did anyone outside the household have access to the trunks?" my friend asked.

Mrs. Bradstreet shook her head. "No one." She forestalled his next question by raising her hand. "And neither Mary, nor Cook, would steal from me. Mary gets my cast-offs to sell as part of her package. The dress would have come to her eventually. She had no need, nor any inclination, to steal."

I perceived that maid and mistress were close. It is a friendship that sometimes arises in smaller households, especially during periods of mourning, when the mistress cannot entertain at home or go out visiting as she would normally do.

Holmes looked around. "I notice that Nathaniel is not here this time."

"Nathaniel has returned to work. He is a tailor. You may have seen his shop. It is on the Marylebone High Street."

Holmes rose to his feet. "I thank you for your time, Mrs. Bradstreet. And yours as well, Mary. You have both been exceedingly helpful."

Mrs. Bradstreet touched my friend's arm lightly. "You will let me know when you find out what happened to my husband, and also to my brother?"

Holmes nodded gravely. "You have my word upon it."

We took our leave and walked out into the late morning sunshine. There was no cab immediately available, and as it was a pleasant morning, we began to walk.

"That was unusual behaviour for Mycroft, was it not?" I asked, after we had walked in silence for some minutes.

Holmes made a non-committal noise. We walked on again in silence. Finally he spoke. "Mycroft and I have very different views on the female of the species."

"I had surmised that after our last visit to the Diogenes Club."

Holmes barked a short dry laugh, completely devoid of any humour. "Yes, that was very telling, was it not?

We continued walking in silence. I kept my eye out for a cab.

"Our mother died when I was five years old," said Holmes suddenly. "I was young enough to accept the sympathy and mothering from our cook and the maids. Mycroft was twelve, and he felt that he was too old for that. He held himself aloof, and has done so ever since. At some level, I believe Mycroft viewed our mother's death as some sort of betrayal, though I doubt he would acknowledge it as such, even to himself. Consequently, he has never allowed himself to get close to another human being, and has certainly never contemplated marriage. He has colleagues, but no friends."

"Neither did you, when I met you," I said. "Nor, as far as I am aware, have you ever contemplated marriage." I stopped talking abruptly, suddenly uncomfortable, wondering if I had said too much. If I had presumed far too much upon our bond of friendship.

Holmes smiled, a little wryly. "You may be assured that it came as a surprise to me, as it no doubt did to you, that we became friends. Though I think you had as many friends as I did. As for the other." He paused. "I would not be a good provider, Watson, and could not, in good faith, ask a woman to share my life. I am far too selfish to make a good husband. Why should I inflict that on an honest woman?"

I was amazed at Holmes' openness with me. We had not spoken like this before. This case was making us both think about our lives and our choices. Whether that was a good thing or not, time alone would tell.

"It is true that I am not the most sociable of men either, I said. "I like a drink, or a game of billiards, or a little flutter, all of which are easily found at a club with minor acquaintances. I also admit to liking the company of women."

Holmes did not reply.

I wondered if that, having been so candid with me, he was now regretting it.

Holmes saw a cab approaching which he proceeded to flag down. Giving the cabbie our address, we settled in for the ride. We sunk deep into our own thoughts, sharing not a word for a goodly length of time.

"Holmes," I said finally. "Do we appraise Lestrade of this new information?"

My friend did not respond at first. When he did respond his voice was low and thoughtful. "Yes, Watson, I believe we shall. I am beginning to form a theory from the data that I have. I am not yet certain where all the pieces fit, or even if they fit at all, but I do think it would be wise to share what we have learned with Lestrade."

"I know better than to ask if you will share your half-formed theory with me." I smiled to show I held no malice.

Holmes gave me a wry glance. "My theory is so absurd that I am not sure that I even want to share it with myself!"

I laughed. "It must be quite absurd then."

"Oh, it is, I assure you."

We lapsed back into silence until we reached Baker Street.

Entering the building we could hear Mrs. Hudson haranguing the butcher's boy in the kitchen. Something about the quality of the chops supplied.

Holmes looked at me. "What do you say to dining at Simpson's this evening, old man?"

"A capital idea, Holmes."

Chapter Seven

We arranged to meet Lestrade at Simpson's that evening. He was waiting for us outside as we strolled up the Strand. "Evening, gentlemen," he said.

"A fine evening, Lestrade. Certainly a fine one for Simpson's roast beef," replied Holmes.

I could see that my friend was in a jovial mood. Associating with Lestrade informally seemed to be improving his temper.

Holmes waited until we were tucking into plates of roast beef, roast vegetables, Yorkshire pudding, and gravy, before telling Lestrade about our day's discovery.

Lestrade listened closely as he methodically chewed his way through Simpson's delicious offering. Nodding occasionally in encouragement. Not that Holmes needed encouragement to talk.

Lestrade placed his knife and fork on his plate, dabbed at his moustache with the napkin, before crumpling the napkin beside his plate. "It is certainly odd, Holmes, but is it connected to the killings?"

"To be frank, Lestrade, I do not know. I have the beginnings of a theory, but as I said to Watson earlier, it is really far too absurd to be taken seriously. However, one thing is for certain: it is an odd theft from an extremely odd household."

"I will grant you that," said Lestrade.

He turned his head sharply as a flash of blue went past the window. Holmes and I followed his gaze to see several uniformed police officers running in one direction, while civilians ran in the other. Some looked excited, some horrified, and some distinctly ill.

Lestrade was already heading towards the door as Holmes and I got to our feet. Holmes threw money for the meal onto the table; we grabbed our coats, and hastened after Lestrade. When we exited the restaurant, Lestrade was already talking to a uniformed sergeant whose shoulder flashes showed he was from A Division.

We reached his side as the sergeant was speaking.

"I don't rightly know how you got here so quickly, Inspector, but I'm right grateful. This is a nasty one."

"I was dining with friends at Simpson's and we noticed the commotion," Lestrade replied. "What has happened, sergeant?"

"It's a woman, sir. Stabbed in the chest."

"You are sure it is a woman?" Holmes asked.

The sergeant, a burly chap of around forty years old, with sandy hair going to gray and mutton-chop whiskers, gave Holmes a shrewd look. "You think it might be connected to the Molly-Boy murders, Mr. Holmes?" he asked.

I was startled by the man's identification of my friend. He saw my look and smiled wryly. "I've seen Mr. Holmes and yourself, Dr. Watson, at the Yard with Inspector Lestrade or Inspector Gregson, many a time."

"Observation is an excellent trait in a police officer," said Holmes.

The sergeant gestured down the street to where a group of constables were blocking off the entrance to an alley. "Come and observe for yourself, sir. If the Inspector don't mind, that is."

"Of course not," said Lestrade. "Mr. Holmes, Doctor Watson." Lestrade gestured for us to accompany him.

We followed the sergeant. My brow was creased in puzzlement. "What is it, Watson?" Holmes asked.

"What on earth is a Molly-Boy?" I asked.

Lestrade chuckled. "Street slang, Doctor Watson. A Molly-Boy is a boy who sells himself while dressed in female clothing. Sometimes known as going on the drag. Most of them operate from around Piccadilly, and are also known as Dilly Boys. The other term is a Piccadilly Rent. As I said they mostly ply their trade around Piccadilly, but also along the Strand and down on the Embankment."

We turned up an alleyway not far from Simpson's. A woman lay on the ground, her clothes an untidy pool around her. Her eyes were half open and she was clearly dead. A knife was angled downwards into her left breast. There was something familiar about her. I drew my breath in sharply as I realized that she looked like Gertrude Swindon.

"Steady, Watson."

"You know who that is?" I asked.

"I know who it looks like," Holmes said. "But I assure you – it is not she." He kneeled down beside the corpse. "Look at the eyes, Watson. They are brown. Mrs. Swindon's eyes are blue."

I kneeled down beside Holmes and saw for myself that what he said was true. The woman bore a strong resemblance to

Gertrude Swindon, but it was not she. I slowly exhaled the breath I had not realized that I was holding in.

Lestrade stood behind us, frowning down. "This almost has to be related to our case." I noted the use of the word 'our'. Usually Lestrade expressed possessiveness over cases, even when he had requested Holmes' help. These murders were obviously getting to the good inspector.

"It could simply be coincidence, Lestrade," I said. I immediately regretted it, given the acerbic look that Holmes turned in my direction.

"I distrust coincidence, Doctor Watson. Especially in the middle of my cases." Lestrade's voice took on a distinctly waspish note.

"Perhaps," I said hurriedly, "We could attend the post-mortem, and then decide what path to take."

Holmes tilted his head slightly in acknowledgement then got to his feet and helped me to mine. We drew back to the mouth of the alleyway and waited patiently for the mortuary van to come for the body, and then followed it back to the morgue.

By the time we arrived at the Royal London the body had been stripped and laid out upon one of the bare, stained, wooden tables. It took me a moment to switch to my professional persona; my mind still being filled with the detritus of the case, and the shock of thinking the corpse was that of someone I had met not too many days past.

Holmes went to examine the woman's clothing, where it lay in a discarded heap in the corner. Lestrade's moustache twitched at the lackadaisical treatment of possible evidence. I joined Doctor Bond at the table. The cause of death was glaringly obvious. A long bladed knife was thrust to the hilt into the woman's left breast. The blade was angled downwards. One quick stroke and it was all over. Little blood would have got on the killer, as the bleeding was almost all internal into the chest cavity, as we discovered when Doctor Bond opened her up.

Holmes came and stood by my side. He raised one of the corpse's hands, examining it closely. "Do you see here, Watson, signs of recent light manual work?"

I followed Holmes' gaze, noting that the tips of her fingers were reddened and starting to spatulate. I looked at Holmes for an explanation.

"The lady had recently began to use a typewriter," he said. "It is similar to the shape of a pianists finger tips, but not so much as to cause confusion."

Holmes looked down at the corpse, his face the dispassionate mask he usually wore during cases.

"This unfortunate woman has recently fallen on hard times," Holmes said. "Her outer clothing is still of good quality and class. Though her underthings are of cheaper material. The corset is stiffened with buckram rather than bone or ivory stays, and her chemise and petticoats are of distinctly inferior quality. These are the things that wear out the most quickly and therefore need replacing more frequently. Her hands tell me she now needed to earn a living for herself, but had not reached the point where she was reduced to selling herself. She had, however, sold her wedding ring." Holmes indicated a slightly lighter band of skin on her left ring finger.

"A widow then," said Lestrade.

"Just so."

Holmes bent to examine the knife that Doctor Bond had removed, and which lay on the table beside the corpse. "Not particularly useful. Any decent cutler in London sells knives like this. Good quality steel. Razor sharp."

"It would need to be, to do with it what he did," I said.

Lestrade shrugged. "You would be amazed at what some people try and kill others with. I once had to deal with a woman who tried to cut her husband's throat with a butter knife. Mind you, she was dead drunk on gin at the time."

"I think we can safely say our killer is not a drunkard. This was a little too well-organized for that," said Holmes, turning away from the table. "Well, Lestrade, is there a place where we may converse privately?"

"If you gentlemen are finished here, we can go to my office at the Yard," he said.

Holmes looked at me. "Watson?"

I nodded. "I have seen enough for tonight."

We thanked Doctor Bond for his time, and his patience, and left the morgue.

By mutual consent we chose to walk to Scotland Yard. The evening air, though full of smoke and the aroma of horse manure, was sweeter than the cloying and caustic smell of the morgue. The thick yellow fog which so plagued the city these days had not yet begun to settle in. Our walk took us through the sounds and bustle of a normal spring evening in London, restoring me to my usual state of equilibrium by the time we had reached Whitehall Place.

Lestrade had a little office tucked away in a corner on the third floor. Far enough from the offices of those further up the chain of command to show that he was not their favourite person. Rumour had it that the office had once belonged to Freddie Abberline.

Lestrade dropped into the chair behind the desk, propping his heels on the top, ankles crossed, and leaned back in the chair. It creaked alarmingly. He gestured for Holmes and I to seat ourselves on the two, somewhat rickety, wooden chairs that sat facing the desk.

"As I see it," Lestrade said. "We have two dead male whores, one dead semi-government agent, and a dead woman who may or may not be connected to the case. If, indeed, the whores and the agent are even connected."

Holmes shook his head. "Those three murders are definitely connected. It is stretching the bounds of possibility far too much to have two killers with the same mode of killing operating in the same area at the same time."

"But we do not know how they are linked," I said.

"No."

"Or why they are linked," said Lestrade

"No."

"Or even if tonight's murder is connected," I said.

"It is connected, all right, Watson. I am unable to see how at this precise moment. But I will."

"The fact is, gentlemen, we know bugger all," said Lestrade. "The more we learn, the less sense it seems to make." The rare expletive from the little detective showed how rattled he was by the case.

"It is indeed a tangled web," said Holmes. His response was almost absent-minded. He was clearly thinking hard.

"This is less the intricate weavings of an arachnid, Mr. Holmes, as a ball of wool after a kitten has finished with it," said Lestrade, with some asperity.

He dug in his drawer and dragged out a silver flask, poured himself a small measure, then waved the flask at me in a silent offer. I smiled and shook my head. Holmes did not even look up. Lestrade shrugged, knocked back his shot, and returned the flask to the drawer.

When Holmes spoke, his voice was soft and measured, as if thinking aloud. "Nancy, the first victim, was a street whore who was known to the second victim. Molly, the second victim, was living with a woman who resembles the fourth victim. It is the third victim, Jeremiah Bradstreet, who does not seem to fit into the pattern. Yet, his death is in the same manner as the first two murders, so he clearly does fit into the pattern."

Lestrade sat up straight, swinging his legs off his desk, placing his feet flat on the floor. He leaned across the desk towards my friend. His face took on a tight, pinched, look of concentration.

"Holmes," Lestrade said, his tone urgent, "Could tonight's killing have been a case of mistaken identity?"

Holmes gave him a sharp look. "The killer thought he had killed Gertrude Swindon?"

"Yes. What if he followed Molly Clutterbuck before the killing? Choosing his place and time. What if he had seen Gertrude Swindon, but not been able to get a really close look?"

"Meaning his targets are primarily the residents of the Cleveland Street house?"

"Yes."

"That is possible, Lestrade." Holmes eyes sparkled with excitement. "Indeed, it is highly probable. The unconnected threads there are Jeremiah Bradstreet, and Nancy, but we can work with that hypothesis of yours. We will make a detective out of you yet."

A thought struck me. "Good God!"

"What is it, Watson?" Holmes turned towards me, brows raised in query.

"What will he do when he finds out he has killed the wrong woman?"

Holmes eyes widened, and then narrowed, as he contemplated my thought. "Mrs. Swindon may very well still be in danger under those circumstances," Holmes said. "And very possibly Sir Lucas as well."

"Sir Lucas?" asked Lestrade.

"Sir Lucas owns the house," said Holmes. "The murderer may also go after the man he perceives as supplying them with shelter."

Lestrade opened his mouth to say something. Holmes held up his hand. "Such knowledge as to who owns what property is quite easily ascertained. It would not take our killer long to find that it belongs to Sir Lucas, and then less time again to find where Sir Lucas resides."

"They must be warned," I said.

Lestrade nodded. "I will go and see Sir Lucas. You two visit Mrs. Swindon. It is, after all, on your way back to Baker Street."

Holmes and I were silent during our ride to Cleveland Street. I was keenly aware of my friend, sunk deep into his thoughts, wrestling with the case before us. I, for one, could not see any hope of solving it, and I suspected that Lestrade felt the same. Only Holmes, I knew, would not give up. He would be like a bulldog with a bone until he had teased the truth out of the sparse facts currently at our disposal.

The cab dropped us outside Mrs. Swindon's house. A quick rap of the knocker brought Gertrude Swindon to the door. Her eyebrows arched elegantly at the sight of us. "Mr. Holmes. Doctor Watson. What an earth brings you to my door at this time of the evening? Have you news on poor Molly?"

My friend's tone was somber. "May we came in, Mrs. Swindon?"

The lady let us in and led us to a comfortably furnished room overlooking Cleveland Street. She settled onto a sofa and looked at us expectantly as we seated ourselves in two armchairs.

"A few hours ago a woman was murdered just off the Strand," said Holmes.

Gertrude nodded. "Dorothy mentioned that. She was out checking on some new ladies we may be able to help."

"Did this Dorothy see the deceased?" I asked.

Gertrude shook her head. "No. She saw all the commotion. She did mention that she saw you gentlemen and Inspector Lestrade at the scene."

Holmes frowned. "Then she will not know the most salient fact about the deceased."

"Which is?" The eyebrows arched in enquiry again.

"The poor woman in question bore an uncanny resemblance to yourself."

Gertrude put her hand to her mouth in shock.

"Inspector Lestrade thinks it is possible that it was a case of mistaken identity," I said.

Mrs. Swindon looked sharply at Holmes. "Do you agree with him?"

"I think it is very possible. We can link two of the victims together, and one of them directly to you. It is not beyond the bounds of possibility that the killer is aware of this house, but labours under the same misapprehension that Lestrade and others did."

"Namely, that I am a bawd."

"Precisely, ma'am."

"Have you seen anyone lurking outside?" I asked.

A charming contralto voice spoke from the doorway. "Given what the house down the other end of the street actually is, there are always people lurking outside. Many of them extremely unsavoury."

We turned to see an attractive young woman entering the room. I rose to my feet politely. Holmes followed suit, a small smile on his face.

It took me a moment to realize that I had met this charming young woman before. It was hard to recognize the diffident Daniel in the confident young woman in front of me, whom I realized must be the Dorothy of whom Gertrude Swindon spoke.

"The house?" I asked.

"It is a notorious boy brothel, Watson. Staffed by telegraph boys in the main. They are going to come to police attention one of these days. There is an extremely nasty scandal brewing along there." said Holmes.

Mrs. Swindon nodded. "My cousin is selling this house and we are moving out towards Kensington, into another that he owns. Hopefully being further away from the temptation of the streets will make it easier for some of our lasses."

I sighed. "So unsavoury characters lurking are ten a penny around here then."

"Some of this country's aristocrats might object to being described as unsavoury," said Holmes, "...but you are, essentially, correct."

"Aristocrats?"

"I did say there was a scandal brewing. Telegraph boys and titled men do not make for a good combination."

I sighed again. "It occurs to me that Mycroft is worrying about entirely the wrong things."

"You are not wrong. That, however, is a thought for another day. We have enough to be dealing with without adding lascivious lords into the mix."

Holmes turned his attention back to Gertrude Swindon. "Mrs. Swindon, is there someone who can act as a protector for you until this man is caught? Once the killer realizes he has made a mistake, I am of the opinion that he will try again."

Gertrude looked thoughtful for a while. "I will ask Luce to send me Jenkins' son, Michael. He works as an ostler for the family. I have known him since he was a child. He is tall and strong, and stands no nonsense."

"An excellent idea. Send for him straight away, but do not, I beg you, go outside alone, or open the door to strangers."

Mrs. Swindon rose to her feet, and we followed. "You have my word, Mr. Holmes. And I thank you both for your warning, and for your consideration of me."

"Not just you," I said. "Inspector Lestrade has gone to warn your cousin."

"You think Luce could be in danger?"

"It is not beyond the bounds of possibility that the killer has tracked down the owner of this house, as well as its inhabitants," said Holmes.

"Well, Luce is surrounded by strong family retainers. I am sure that he, at least will be fine."

Smiling graciously, Gertrude Swindon showed us to the door. We took our leave of her and Dorothy, and headed out into the night and back to the comfort of our rooms.

Once home I pottered around getting myself ready for sleep. To my surprise I heard the door to our rooms open and shut softly. I hurried out in time to hear the street door close.

Looking out of the window I saw Holmes striding purposefully away down the street. I hesitated for a moment, torn between wishing to accompany him, and the need for sleep. Sleep won out. I knew that if Holmes had wanted me with him, he would have said. There were things, I knew, that were best done unaccompanied. I headed off to bed, mentally wishing Holmes good hunting, whatever, or whomever, his quarry was.

Chapter Eight

I had finished breakfast and was reading the first of the morning newspapers, when Holmes dragged himself up the stairs. He looked exhausted, elated, and frustrated, in equal measures.

Dropping into his chair he asked, "Is there any breakfast left?"

I rang for Mrs. Hudson, who, with minimal grumbling, supplied Holmes with fresh bacon, eggs, toast, and a pot of coffee. He gave her a tired smile as he sat at the table to eat. I noted the look of exasperated affection she gave him, but said nothing. Holmes, for all his comments on not having friends, did have people who cared about him and whom he cared about in return, for all that he denied it.

Finally replete, Holmes poured the last of his coffee into his cup, and came to sit opposite me in his armchair.

"Was it a successful night?" I asked.

"Not particularly. I have been chasing down every rumour and possible sighting of our killer that I could. I have learned many things, but as yet, I have no way of knowing what is useful, and what is merely the babble of those who dwell upon the streets."

"What did you learn?"

"That the killer is a short man, a tall man, a fat man, and also a skinny one." Holmes' tone was sour.

"Useful skill for a killer to have." My tone was bland.

Holmes gave me an enquiring look.

"Being able to change his shape like that."

Holmes let out a humourless bark of laughter. "Eye-witnesses are the worst thing a detective can encounter, Watson. Whether they mean to or not, they tend to tell you what they think you wish to hear, or what conforms with what they have already heard, or they embroider their story to make it sound more interesting."

"From that I take it you ran into a few eye-witnesses last night."

"One or two. The majority of them were of the "a friend told me that they saw" variety of informant." Holmes' tone was dry and weary.

"Did you learn anything substantive?"

"Several people spoke of seeing a man with a doctor's bag."

I winced. "Shades of the Whitechapel killer come back to haunt us." During the previous year's panic it had been dangerous for any doctor to go into Whitechapel with his bag. He took his life into his hands each time he did so.

"It is only natural, Watson. The police never caught that killer. He is going to come to mind every time there is a killing even vaguely similar for the next twenty or thirty years. Until the memory of the killings dies away."

"If they ever do."

"They will. Everything dies eventually. Even you and I."

"You are getting unnecessarily morbid for this time of the morning, Holmes."

"My apologies, my good Watson. I am tired and more than a little dispirited. Apart from our Jack the Ripper lookalike, people have seen mysterious carriages where they have no right to be, an exceptionally tall woman wearing a dark hooded cloak, a soldier carrying a blood stained knife, and three people solemnly assured me that they had seen Jesus Christ walking upon the Thames!"

"What?" I could not keep my incredulous disbelief from showing in my voice.

Holmes gave me a slight, somewhat pained, smile. "If I learned nothing else I have learned that it is pointless attempting to have conversations with drunks on the Victoria Embankment at 3 a.m."

I could not help but laugh at that.

Holmes was fighting back yawns. I took the cup from his hand. "Get some sleep. You need it."

Nodding, Holmes got his feet and meandered his drowsy way to his bedroom. The door closed with a definite thud.

I tidied up the breakfast dishes before ringing for Mrs. Hudson to remove them. Then I settled back down with my newspapers and my morning pipe.

I think I sat reading for a couple of hours, before Mrs. Hudson knocked on the door. She stuck her head into the room. "Doctor Watson, there is a police constable here."

"Send him in, please, Mrs. Hudson." I folded my papers and laid them aside.

A young police constable edged nervously into the room. God knows what he had been told about my friend. Possibly that he eats young coppers for breakfast. Lestrade had a distinctly perverse sense of humour at times. I almost wanted to tell the constable that Holmes had already dined and that he was in no danger.

The lad swallowed hard. He was painfully young; his uniform so new it damn near squeaked.

"Inspector Lestrade sends his regards, Doctor Watson, and requests the presence of yourself and Mr. Holmes at Sir Lucas Catterick's house in Kensington. There has been an attempt on Sir Lucas' life."

I sprang to my feet. "Wait here, lad. I will rouse Holmes."

I hurried into Holmes' room. I called his name from the doorway. A grumbling noise answered me.

"Lestrade needs our help."

Holmes stuck his head out of the blankets and gave me a cross look. "Lestrade needs all the help he can get."

"There has been an attempt on Sir Lucas' life."

The change in Holmes was dramatic. One moment half asleep; the next wide awake and leaping out of bed, and reaching for fresh clothing.

I returned to the sitting room to wait. The constable was lurking by the door as if he expected everything in the room to attack him, myself not excluded. After a moment's thought, I went and fetched my bag. Lestrade had said it was an attempt, so maybe I would be able to assist.

Holmes soon joined us and the three of us departed to Kensington in a cab. The constable could provide no further information, even when questioned by Holmes. After a while, Holmes gave up in disgust, and gazed broodingly out of the window.

The constable guarding the door of Sir Lucas' house opened it as soon as he saw us alight from the cab. A harassed looking Lestrade came out to greet us. He glanced at my bag. "You will not need that, Doctor."

"There are no injuries?" asked Holmes, surprised.

"Not to Sir Lucas," said Lestrade.

Both Holmes and I caught the tone, and the anger, in Lestrade's voice.

"What happened?" asked Holmes, his voice sharp.

"Sir Lucas and his secretary, Thomas Arbuthnot, had gone to the house in Cleveland Street to make sure the property was secure. The killer was inside the house. He attacked Sir Lucas with a knife. Arbuthnot shoved Sir Lucas out of the way."

"How badly hurt is Arbuthnot?" I asked.

Lestrade gave me a sad smile. "As I said, Doctor Watson, you will not need your bag."

"Dead," said Holmes, his tone flat.

"As a doornail," Lestrade affirmed.

I thought of the Scotsman's gentle touch on Sir Lucas' shoulder when we had visited here before. The obvious affection between the two men. I hefted my bag. "I may still need this. Take me to Sir Lucas."

Jenkins materialized behind Lestrade. "This way, please, Doctor Watson." The butler's eyes were red rimmed. It seemed Arbuthnot was well-liked within the household. I followed him upstairs to the master bedroom.

Sir Lucas was collapsed on the bed. His mother hovered at his bedside, and I noted the presence of Gertrude Swindon. The ladies looked up as I entered behind Jenkins.

Lady Amelia gave me a grateful little smile. "Doctor Watson, how good of you to come." She spotted my bag. "You are here to help Luce?"

"If I can."

Lady Amelia stepped back from the bedside, allowing me to take her place. Sir Lucas looked up at me, his face a mask of shock, and his eyes filled with terrible pain. I had seen such reactions to the loss of close comrades on the battlefield. I looked down at him gravely. "Sir Lucas."

"You have heard?"

I nodded. "Inspector Lestrade sent for Holmes and myself immediately." I was aware of Holmes and Lestrade in the hallway outside the door.

Sir Lucas grasped my wrist, in much the same way his grandmother had done. "He came out of the front parlour, screaming my name. Called me a pimp and a whoremonger, and came at me with a knife. Thomas..." He paused, and swallowed hard. "Thomas shoved me out of the way, but in doing so took the blade himself. In the throat. The noise alerted the coachman who came into the house. The madman swore, glared at me, shoved the coachman aside, and ran out into the street."

"In which direction?" Holmes asked from his place in the doorway.

"I am sorry, but I did not notice. I was too busy trying to help Thomas." A spasm of grief passed across Sir Lucas" face.

"I know that this is extremely painful for you, Sir Lucas. But I must ask – did you manage to get a good look at the man?" Holmes' voice was gentle.

"Not as good as I would have liked," Sir Lucas said. "Nothing about him stood out. He wore a plain black scarf high up across his face, probably to hide his features. A simple suit of dark material such as any clerk or merchant would wear. He had a soft cloth cap on his head." Sir Lucas' voice was becoming firmer and more sure, as he realized that Holmes was the best chance he had of catching Arbuthnot's murderer. "I noticed he was slightly shorter than Thomas. So maybe around six feet tall."

Lestrade gave Holmes a look of enquiry. Holmes nodded. Lestrade's moustache twitched in response, and he ran down the stairs bellowing for his officers.

Remembering our conversation at Cleveland Street about unsavoury characters in the street, I sighed. The chances of anyone having seen the killer were unlikely in the extreme.

Holmes looked at me. "It is possible that someone saw something, Watson. A man running down Cleveland Street would be very likely to catch people's attention. People visiting that street do tend to be reluctant to draw attention to themselves."

I looked at him and thought about this for a moment. "Meaning most visitors to that street skulk rather than run."

"Exactly!"

I looked away from Holmes and down at my patient. "You need rest, Sir Lucas. You have been attacked, and a fine young man sacrificed his life for yours. You will need to be well rested to deal with everything that is to come."

I looked at Lady Amelia. "Do you have laudanum in the house?"

"Of course."

"I do not usually recommend opiates, but under the circumstances, I suggest giving Sir Lucas a small dose of laudanum, and allowing him to sleep."

I looked Lady Amelia in the eyes and added "If he shows excessive grief for the death of a man who to all intents and purposes was a servant, people will notice. And people being what they are, they will also gossip."

Lady Amelia nodded, understanding immediately what I meant. Then she said "Before you and Mr. Holmes leave, would you call in on my mother, doctor? I think she could use your reassurance."

"We both will," Holmes said, somewhat to my surprise.

It was Gertrude Swindon who escorted us down the corridor to Lady Caroline's room, before returning to Sir Lucas' bedside.

To my surprise, Dorothy was seated beside the old lady's bed, reading to her from a copy of Strand Magazine. They both looked up as we entered.

Holmes walked across and raised Lady Caroline's hand in his, bowing over it like the gentleman he truly was. "Sherlock Holmes at your service, Lady Caroline. I just wished to assure you that Doctor Watson and I will do our best, along with Inspector Lestrade, to find the murderer of your grandson's friend and companion."

"Thank you, Mr. Holmes." She looked across at me. "And thank you, Doctor Watson, I know that we can rely on you both. But surely you cannot want to speak with me about the events. I was not even there."

"Your daughter is concerned for you, Lady Caroline," I said. "She asked me to look on you before we left. Holmes just came along for the pleasure of your company."

Lady Caroline laughed a crackly laugh, which put colour in her cheeks and left her slightly breathless.

"You made quite an impression on my friend," said Holmes. "Naturally I desired to meet you."

I stepped up to the bedside and took her wrist in my hand. The pulse was steady. No cause for alarm there. I gave Lady Caroline a reassuring smile. "We will do our best to find Arbuthnot's killer."

She nodded. "I know that you will. Until he is caught, Luce will be in danger."

The perspicuous old lady had got right to the heart of the matter. Until the killer was apprehended, Sir Lucas, and Gertrude Swindon, would both be in considerable danger. Newspapers would soon be reporting the names of the victims, and he would know he had made ghastly mistakes. Though in the case of Thomas Arbuthnot, the killer was already aware of his failure.

We graciously took our leave of Lady Caroline and returned to Sir Lucas' bedroom. Lestrade was waiting just inside the door. He nodded when he saw us. Sir Lucas was drowsing; it was obvious that Lady Amelia had administered the laudanum as per my instructions. Lestrade spoke softly to her.

"I am leaving men outside the house to keep watch. If they see anything untoward they will act."

Lady Amelia thanked him graciously and turned back to her son. Gertrude came to escort us to the front door.

"Are you returning home, Mrs. Swindon?" asked Holmes, "Because, I could not, in all good conscience recommend that particular course of action."

"No. Dorothy and I will remain here. I had asked Luce for someone to guard the house and he suggested that Dorothy and I come here instead. I have no other lodgers at this time. With all that has been happening, it has not felt safe to bring new girls in. Now even less so."

Holmes nodded gravely. "With Lestrade's men outside you should be safe in here."

"I have Constable Braddon guarding the kitchen door. He is a keen amateur boxer. No-one will get past him," Lestrade said.

Gertrude smiled. "I saw him. Cook has taken a shine to him. When I saw him he was sitting at the kitchen table being plied with tea and cake."

Lestrade twitched his moustache in amusement. "He will be a happy man then."

Jenkins appeared to open the door for us, and, taking our leave, we hastened out into the street.

Lestrade turned to Holmes. "On to Cleveland Street?"

"Of course." My friend's tone was slightly testy, as if annoyed and surprised that Lestrade even needed to ask. Lestrade rolled his eyes, and signaled to one of his constables to acquire a cab.

The journey to Cleveland Street was conducted in silence. Both Lestrade and I knew better than to intrude on Holmes' thoughts.

A constable stood on guard at the top of the steps. We hurried past him and into the house. Holmes stopped just inside the doorway, turning back to give the lock a cursory glance, causing Lestrade and I to bump into him.

The scent of blood was sharp in the air. A less than savoury meaty smell, overlaid with the tang of iron. Blood was pooled on the floor just outside the front parlour, and sprayed up the wall and the door frame. Holmes drew his magnifying glass from his pocket and began to carefully survey the scene.

I stood beside Lestrade. I was strangely reluctant to gaze upon the site of the death of a young man I had so recently met and liked. Lestrade, seeing more than enough death in the course of his duties, was content to stand with me in quiet companionship.

Eventually Holmes straightened up and tucked his glass away. "There is one thing, Lestrade, the killer will not have been able to escape getting blood on him this time. It is obvious from the pattern of the blood upon the wall that he hit an artery."

Lestrade nodded. "I have men out questioning householders and passersby. With luck someone will have spotted something."

"Evidence is vastly preferable to luck. You can, at least, present evidence in a courtroom." Holmes tone was sour.

I looked around at our surroundings, which now more resembled a slaughterhouse than a home. "Have we finished here?"

"Not quite. I have yet to discover the killer's means of entry. The windows are intact at the front, as was the lock."

Someone close by cleared their throat.

We looked around to see a uniformed sergeant with greying mouse-brown hair and an abashed expression, standing in the doorway that led back into the domestic area of the house.

He shuffled a little uncomfortably under the scrutiny. "Begging your pardon, Mr. Holmes, Inspector Lestrade, but there's damage in the kitchen. Window near the door has been broken."

He flicked a glance at Lestrade. "I thought someone should have a look around, Inspector, just in case the killer wasn't alone."

Holmes gave him an approving look. "Well done, sergeant. Lead on."

We followed the sergeant into the kitchen. Glass from a broken window next to the door lay on the floor. The door itself was unlocked, and ajar, gently moving in the slight breeze.

Holmes hurried across to examine the scene for himself, taking careful stock of the broken window and the door.

Lestrade cast a glance around the room, frowning slightly. "I do not think much of Mrs. Swindon's domestic arrangements. There is dust on the table and traces of dirt in the corners."

Holmes turned his head, eyebrows raised in vaguely amused enquiry. "Since when did you worry about the domestic arrangements of others, Lestrade? May I remind you that you do not have a kitchen?"

"Neither do you," Lestrade shot back, slightly stung. "But I cannot see your Mrs. Hudson letting her kitchen get in such a state."

Holmes looked at Lestrade thoughtfully, turning the comment over in his mind. "An excellent point, Lestrade. You could eat off the floor of our esteemed landlady's kitchen. Not that she would let you, of course."

Holmes looked around the room and frowned slightly. "I can see no sign that Mrs. Swindon has domestics. The dirt in the corners, for example. Good staff know how to get that out with minimum fuss. And, of course, no cook would allow her benches and tables to get in such a state. Nor would a plate be left out." He pointed to where a fine china plate sat forlornly on the table.

I frowned. "Maybe Mrs. Swindon could not afford domestics."

Lestrade almost laughed. "With Sir Lucas footing the bill?"

"I was not thinking of it in monetary terms," I said, lowering my voice so the sergeant could not overhear. "More that she may not have felt that she could trust strangers with the secrets of the house."

Both Holmes and Lestrade stared at me for a moment, then Lestrade shoot a look at Holmes, as if asking what he thought of the idea.

"You may have something with that theory, my dear Watson," said Holmes, softly. "Strangers would leave her open to blackmail, at the very least."

Lestrade nodded his agreement. "There is something else that has just occurred to me. Mrs. Swindon would need to train her girls in household management."

Holmes and I gave him equally blank looks.

Lestrade chuckled. "I take it neither of you gentlemen have sisters? My mother taught my sisters how to cook, and clean, and sew, and all other manner of household tasks. Starting when they were about four or five years old. The likes of Dorothy would have no idea how to do these tasks and would need to be taught.

It was the turn of Holmes and I to exchange looks.

"You have thought about this a lot, have you not, Lestrade?" Holmes said.

Lestrade shrugged. "Once you told me what was happening here, I found myself thinking about the details."

Holmes nodded approvingly. I noted that Lestrade preened himself a little.

"What are your conclusions on the broken window, Holmes?" I asked.

Holmes turned back to the window and door. He gestured at the glass on the floor. "Obviously broken from the outside, otherwise the pieces of glass would not be on the floor on the inside. The murderer broke this window because it allowed him to get entry via the door. You can see the key is still within the lock. Most people do have a tendency to leave the key in the lock. Very unsafe, especially with a window so close to the door. The killer reached in and turned the key, thereby opening the door for himself. The door was probably left open to allow him to leave silently the way he arrived. He was obviously searching the place for its occupants when Sir Lucas and Thomas Arbuthnot arrived."

Holmes' face fell into a somber expression. "Realizing that he could not get out the way he came in; he attacked Sir Lucas. No doubt thinking that getting another of the people he was after would do as well."

"But he did not," I said, my voice shaking slightly.

"No," Holmes agreed. "He murdered a brave, honourable, and innocent man instead."

Silence fell between us. The sergeant shuffled uncomfortably.

Lestrade cleared his throat. "Are we finished here?"

Holmes glanced around. "I think we have seen all that is useful here. Time we attended the mortuary."

"Where did they take him?" I asked Lestrade.

"Not far. Just to the Middlesex."

I should have realized that, as I had noticed the hospital's annex in this street the first time we visited. A visit that seemed an impossibly long time ago.

We walked in silence through the house, out the front door, and on to the hospital.

When we arrived, we followed Lestrade down cold, dank, corridors to the small morgue in the basement. The Middlesex was primarily a teaching hospital, though not as old, or as prestigious, as Barts or Guys. It had a well-appointed, modern morgue that occasionally did service as a police morgue. Though it rarely saw as many violent death corpses as either Barts or the Royal London.

Thomas Arbuthnot's body had been stripped and was laid out on a table on the right hand side of the room. It was clear from the state of the corpse that the post-mortem had yet to begin. Apart from the ghastly wound to the throat, the body was untouched.

Holmes bent over the body, examining the wound closely with the aid of his glass. I stood back. The feeling of reluctance I had at the house was even stronger here. Lestrade stood beside me, content to let Holmes have his head.

Holmes stretched, sighed, shook his head, and came across to us, tucking his glass into his pocket as he came. "A bad business. The young fellow had no chance. The knife blade entered his throat just below the larynx in a downward movement, then slid sideways and exited the left hand side of his neck, severing the carotid artery as it did so. Hence the amount of blood upon the walls, and, no doubt, upon the killer."

Holmes walked towards the door.

"If he is sprayed with blood, then perhaps someone will report him to the police," I said, following closely behind Holmes. I had been thinking about this since Holmes' comment at the house.

Lestrade was morose. "I would not get my hopes up, doctor. They are as cliquish around here as they are in the East End, and no more likely to tell the police anything. Only time they call the police around here is when trouble comes in from other areas."

"As indeed it has today," said Holmes, with a hint of acid in his voice. He then shook himself like a ruffled cat. "Come, Watson, Lestrade, we are letting the case get to us. Time to sit down and discuss it in a civilized manner. Over some of Mrs. Hudson's excellent tea and crumpets."

By mutual, though unspoken, consent, we walked back to Baker Street.

Not only did Mrs. Hudson supply tea and crumpets, but also scones with jam and cream. And a pot of coffee as well as one of tea.

Mrs. Hudson left, leaving us to eat and to discuss the case in peace. Silence reigned for a while, as we all turned our attention to the excellent repast we had been provided with.

Finally, Lestrade picked up his napkin, dabbed a blob of cream from off his moustache, and sat back in his chair with a contented sigh. "Time to talk, gentlemen?" he asked.

Holmes placed his cup back in his saucer, and turned his attention to Lestrade.

I took another bite from my crumpet before turning my own attention to the inspector.

Lestrade picked up his tea cup and took a sip. "Our killer definitely knows he got the wrong person near Simpson's."

I gave Lestrade an enquiring look around my mouthful of crumpet.

"Just before I was called to Arbuthnot's murder I had a chance to glance at the newspapers. Our unfortunate corpse had been identified in them. Those damn reporters work quickly. We had only found out late last night who she was."

"And who was she?" asked Holmes.

"A Mrs. Evelyn Smythe. She was a widow, as you said, Holmes. Husband dropped dead in the street three months ago. Heart attack, I believe. Left her with a large house, four children, and several servants. None of which she could afford. The Smythes were living above their means by quite a considerable amount." Lestrade took another sip of his tea.

"What happened?" I asked.

"Dismissed the servants and sold the house," Lestrade said. "Not that she saw much of the money. Too many outstanding debts. Moved with the children into a small set of rooms not far from here. The eldest girl has got a position as a domestic to the vicar in the parish they had lived in. He and his wife were well-aware of the situation and had been trying to help for some time. His wife promised to look after the girl. The eldest boy has just started at the telegraph office. Between them they were hoping to earn enough to keep the two youngest at a good school. Rebuild the family fortunes that way."

Lestrade put his cup down and looked at us sadly. "She was a very determined lady, from all accounts. Learned to type and got a job as a type-writer at a small lawyer's office close to the Strand. Her husband was a lawyer's clerk, and his employers took her on out of compassion. That is where she was coming from when she was murdered."

"What will happen to the children now?" I asked, my voice full of concern.

Lestrade shrugged. "God knows. The girl has her position with room and board, so she, at least, is safe. The eldest boy does not earn enough to keep the two youngest in school, let alone pay the rent on the rooms. I suspect he will move into a boarding house, and the two young ones will have to go into a workhouse. There is no other family who can take them."

"That is monstrous!" I cried.

Lestrade shrugged, somewhat sadly, I thought. "I did not make the world, doctor. I only try and live in it."

He got to his feet. "Thank you for the tea, gentlemen. I need to be going."

Lestrade put on his coat and reached for his hat. He paused, turning his hat in his hands. "Will I see you gentlemen at Arbuthnot's funeral? Assuming we are invited."

My friend nodded gravely. "Of course."

Lestrade shot us both a small, sad, smile. "I shall be pleased to have your company at such an unhappy occasion."

"We will be there," I assured him.

Dipping his head to us in acknowledgement, Lestrade put on his hat and headed out the door.

Holmes picked up his violin, and, standing at the window, watching Lestrade trudge away, began to play melancholy airs. I took myself to my room, the sadness in the room behind me was almost too much for me to bear. Would we ever find this damn killer, who had ruined so many lives, and, all uncaring, destroyed the futures of four young people? I am not a vengeful man, but that night I found myself praying that this demon incarnate be caught and hanged.

Chapter Nine

The next few days saw Holmes in a frenzy of activity as he once again chased down every person he could think of who could possibly help.

Wiggins from the Baker Street Irregulars firmly promised that he would keep an eye on the Cleveland Street house. Just in case the killer returned to the scene of the crime. Holmes did not think that this was likely, but he appreciated Wiggins' commitment.

When I commented on Wiggins' fervour, Holmes pointed out that the Irregulars lived on the streets. They knew the victims, if only by sight.

"Of course they are going to help, Watson." Holmes' tone was testy. "If for no other reason than the fact that one day someone could start killing street arabs. They know it could quite easily be one of them on the business end of that damn butcher's knife."

It was a day or so after that conversation that Dorothy paid a visit to Baker Street. Dressed in discreet mourning, she settled herself on our little sofa, after handing invitations to the funeral to us both. "Sir Lucas wishes to know if you gentlemen, and Inspector Lestrade, would be pall-bearers?"

I gaped at her. "Sir Lucas wants us to be pall-bearers?"

"It is not an unreasonable request when you consider it, Watson," Holmes said. "It demonstrates a not inconsiderable respect for the deceased."

Dorothy nodded. "Sir Lucas wishes to honour Thomas. Thomas had no family, and died saving Sir Lucas' life. He thinks if the great Sherlock Holmes, Doctor Watson, and Inspector Lestrade are pall-bearers, along with himself, his brother, and Jenkins, it will send the message that Thomas' sacrifice is respected, and also send the message that the killer will be punished."

Holmes raised his eyebrows. "Sir Lucas said this?"

Dorothy raised her left shoulder in a little shrug. "Not in so many words. Gertude knows how his mind works better than he does, I think. She is the one who explained it to me."

Holmes looked thoughtful. "It is a good idea, regardless of motive. It would give us a chance to check the mourners. Our killer may take the opportunity to strike again."

"God, I hope not!" I muttered.

I turned to Dorothy. "Where is the funeral being held?"

"At Kensal Green. Sir Lucas has purchased a special plot for Thomas. The cortege will leave from the house in Kensington. Sir Lucas asks if you will be at the house an hour before we depart."

"Of course we will," Holmes assured her.

"Have you delivered Lestrade's invitation?" I asked. I was wondering how long before the inspector turned up on our doorstep to discuss the matter.

Dorothy shook her head. "Gertrude is delivering that one. I have no desire to venture too close to Scotland Yard, many policemen being what they are, and Sir Lucas did not think it was advisable."

I could not forebear smiling slightly. "Lestrade may have some explaining to do to his fellow officers. Given what the police believe Mrs. Swindon to be."

The smile returned to Dorothy's voice. "I believe that may have been at least part of Gertrude's reason for volunteering. She also knows that they dare not touch her. I, on the other hand, may not have been that fortunate."

Dorothy rose gracefully from the sofa. "Thank you for your time gentlemen. I will tell Sir Lucas that you accept."

I hastened to hold the door open for her. She paused and looked back at us. "You gentlemen have been concerned about my welfare, and that of Gertrude. We have resolved to remain with Sir Lucas until the killer has been caught. Sir Lucas has engaged me to be the companion to Lady Caroline."

Holmes smiled, "Having met that redoubtable lady, I have no doubt you will find it an interesting occupation."

Dorothy laughed gently and took her leave of us.

Holmes walked to the window and watched Dorothy go down the steps of the house and enter the carriage parked at the kerb. He turned back towards me with a half-smile. "Well, Watson, what do you make of that?"

"I am not sure what to make of it, to be honest, Holmes. On one hand it is an excellent idea. On the other, it will scandalize half of London."

"Only half?" Holmes tone held a note of slight amusement.

"Probably more than half," I conceded. "Sir Lucas' own circle and class will accept it, because they will understand how unique the situation is." I sat down in my chair and looked up at Holmes. "What I am really afraid of is that it will draw attention to the relationship that existed between Sir Lucas and

Arbuthnot. I like Sir Lucas. I do not want to see him ostracized and pilloried by the papers and the public."

Holmes dropped casually into his own chair. "Neither do I, and I do not believe such a thing will happen."

"You do not?" I asked.

Holmes shook his head. "No. In the first instance, I think Lady Amelia will rein in any histrionic tendencies in her son. In the second instance, I think that you overestimate the general public's abilities to observe and reason. We know about Sir Lucas and Arbuthnot, therefore we see the pattern of their relationship."

I nodded thoughtfully.

Holmes continued speaking. "Viewed through the eyes of the press, the majority of people will see only the funeral of a man who died heroically to save another. The fact that the man he saved was a baronet, and his employer, is neither here nor there."

Holmes reached for the slipper that held his tobacco. He filled his pipe, lit it, and leaned back comfortably in his chair. "If, indeed, the papers bother to cover it," he said. "People die in London every day, some of them doing heroic things. There was a brief mention in this morning's Times of a man who jumped in the Thames to save a child. It was a small item. A brief snippet of life in a city that places a fairly low value on human life."

"I am not sure if I find that comforting or disturbing." My expression was sour and I knew it.

"I am not actually sure that it was meant to be either, to be honest with you."

"And you are always unfailingly honest with me."

"Sarcasm, Watson?"

"Maybe just a smidgeon," I admitted.

Holmes' eyes sparked with gentle amusement. I marveled, not for the first time, at the strength of our friendship that allowed for banter that other men would take to be unpardonable insults.

The opening of the street door, and voices in the hallway, let us know that Lestrade had arrived.

"Come in, Lestrade," Holmes called out, not bothering to rise from his chair.

"How did you know it was me?" Lestrade asked, coming in the door and shedding his hat and coat.

"By dint of long familiarity I can recognize both your dulcet tones and your delicate tread upon the stair."

Lestrade smiled, and took a seat.

"You had a visitor at Scotland Yard this morning, Lestrade," said Holmes, eyes twinkling with mischief. "A woman. Well-known to you. Caused quite a stir in the building."

"How the devil did you know that?"

"We also had a visitor," I said. "Dorothy. She told us that Gertrude Swindon was calling on you."

"Watson!" Holmes' tone held the barest hint of note of complaint.

Lestrade chuckled. "Mrs. Swindon caused quite a stir, I can tell you. Policemen gossip worse than old women, or sailors, come to that. There is no-one quite like a sailor for supplying information. By the time I left the Yard to come here

I heard that I was living off immoral earnings, that I was about to marry the said Mrs. Swindon, and that she had come to confess to murder."

"You do not seem to be particularly worried about the gossip." I said.

Lestrade shrugged. "Last week I heard that Athelney Jones was spotted in a brothel in Bishopsgate, that the Commissioner is the illegitimate son of a royal Duke, and that Gregson is going to retire to Somerset and breed pigs. None of which is true, well, except maybe the one about Jones, but that raid was pretty quiet due to the fact Royalty was involved, I understand. So the gossip does not worry me, Doctor Watson."

He looked at Holmes. "Now, about this funeral. I take it you have both agreed to be pall-bearers, as I have?"

"Between the three of us we should be able to get a good look at those present. Not so much the guests, but those that turn up to gaze upon the spectacle," said Holmes.

"Do you think many will?" I asked.

"Oh yes," said Lestrade. "It is amazing who you can spot at things like funerals, or fires, for that matter. Gregson caught a housebreaker he had been hunting for months. The idiot came to watch a nearby house fire. Nabbed him clean as a whistle."

"What does one wear as a pall-bearer? I asked, never having performed such a function;
my brother having died whilst I was in India.

"Darkest suit you have and a mourning armband. Now that we are going to be pall-bearers, we need to get armbands on as soon as possible," said Lestrade, who was obviously an old hand at this.

"I believe Watson and I will make a quick visit to Jays," Holmes said. "Neither he nor I own one. A glaring oversight, I know, but neither of us has a large enough circle of genuine friends to warrant keeping such an item. Do you wish to accompany us, Lestrade?"

Lestrade shook his head. "I already have one. I will call in to my rooms and pick it up." He gave a sour smile. "Policemen always need mourning armbands. Too many get killed in the line of duty for us not to keep one."

Lestrade took a cab back to Scotland Yard, and Holmes and I headed for Jays Mourning Warehouse which was located on Regent Street.

I had not known what to expect from an enterprise that existed purely to sell garments and decorations associated with death. I was taken aback by the size of the place. It covered almost a full block of Regent Street. The service was friendly and efficient, and Holmes and I soon left, each with a black silk band around our right arms.

The morning of Thomas Arbuthnot's funeral dawned cool and, thankfully, clear. Holmes and I alighted from a cab outside the house in Kensington, just as Lestrade arrived in another.

A fine glass-sided hearse with six black horses, with black dyed ostrich plumes upon their heads, stood in the street. Two grooms clad in black frock coats stood by the horses.

Several elegant mourning carriages waited further up the street, which was strewn with straw to muffle the sound of the hearse upon the cobbles.

The door knocker was muffled with black crepe, and a wreath of yew, bedecked with black silk ribbons, hung upon the door. Jenkins must have been watching for us, as the door opened before we could knock.

Voices could be heard in the front parlour, as well as a knocking noise. It took me a moment to realize that this was the sound of the undertakers nailing down the lid of the coffin for Arbuthnot's final journey.

Jenkins conducted us upstairs to where Sir Lucas was waiting in a small library. Another man stood with him. His resemblance to Sir Lucas spoke of their relationship. Sir Lucas introduced him as his younger brother, David.

David shook our hands, "A terrible business this. We are all most distressed. Thomas was like family. I am pleased that you gentlemen have agreed to be pall-bearers for him." He shot a sympathetic glance at Sir Lucas. "It helps Luce to know that you are seeking Thomas' killer. I was afraid he would set out to do it himself, and that would never do. But mother persuaded him to leave it in your capable hands."

Lestrade's voice was soft. "We are doing everything that we can. Though with few leads, it is a hard task."

"But you will not give up?" David Catterick's tone was anxious. Lestrade shook his head.

Holmes held up a reassuring hand. "If Scotland Yard decides not to pursue the case, I give you my pledge that I will continue the hunt."

"Thank you, Mr. Holmes. That gives me a great deal of peace." He smiled at us, and moved to his brother's side, where a valet was fastening a mourning band around Sir Lucas" arm.

Lady Amelia appeared in the doorway. "We are almost ready to depart. Gertrude and Dorothy are getting mother into the carriage. Has a bath chair been arranged for mother at the chapel?"

David smiled at his mother. "Jenkins attended to it. I believe Michael took grandmother's chair to the chapel in a cart an hour or so ago. He will wait and bring it back after the service."

"I really do not know what we would do without Jenkins and Michael," Lady Amelia observed. "This house just does not run smoothly without a Jenkins involved somewhere."

Sir Lucas gave a tight little smile. "I swear you make that comment every day, mother. And have done since I was a child."

It was obvious to me that this light, inconsequential, chatter was simply to keep Sir Lucas' mind occupied. Though the look that briefly flickered across my friend's face told me it was annoying him.

Lady Amelia swept out of the room, and we followed her down the stairs in a solemn procession. Jenkins waited for us at the door to the parlour, along with the undertaker.

We filed silently into the room and arranged ourselves around the coffin. Holmes and Lestrade made sure that I was between them, so that the weight would not be too onerous upon my shoulder. Hefting our tragic burden, we shuffled out of the room, then out of the house to where the hearse sat. The undertaker's men assisted us as we loaded the coffin in gently, and then rearranged the flowers around it.

The undertaker escorted us to the lead carriage, which would go before the hearse to Kensal Green. Looking back I saw Lady Amelia joining Lady Caroline, Gertrude, and Dorothy in the carriage reserved for the chief mourners. Several people I took to be servants were entering secondary carriages. It was clear that Sir Lucas intended as fine a farewell as possible for Thomas Arbuthnot.

The ride to Kensal Green was blessedly short. Sir Lucas sat straight backed and silent for the duration.

A tall, cadaverous figure, with a sharp nose, silver hair, and clad in vicar's garments waited outside the chapel. He looked, to me, like something out of Dickens. Lestrade must have thought so too, as he whispered "Uriah Heep" to himself. I could not help but agree, though that character had been a lawyer rather than a vicar.

The chapel itself, though a Church of England establishment, would have been more suited to the rites of Zeus or Athena, than those of God, as Englishmen perceive Him to be. Made mostly of Portland Stone, its colonnade of Doric columns was an inspiring sight, and had been quite the talk of the town when the cemetery first opened.

Standing to the right hand side of the portico was a young man holding the handles of a bath chair. I took this young man to be Jenkins' son, Michael, indeed, he had the look of his father about him. He wheeled the chair carefully towards the carriage directly behind the hearse. The vicar hurried to attend to the ladies, and help settle Lady Caroline in her chair, as we exited our carriage and stood beside the door of the hearse.

The other mourners left their vehicles and hurried into the chapel to be guided to their appointed seats by two gentlemen ushers supplied by the undertaking firm.

Having seen Lady Caroline comfortably settled and escorted inside, the vicar gave the undertaker a nod, before turning on his heel and sweeping into the chapel. We again shouldered our burden and followed him in. Once the coffin was laid before the altar, we took our own seats close to the ladies of the household.

I must admit to finding church services unutterably dull. Holmes' eyes flicked quickly around taking in our surroundings and the people present, and Lestrade paid attention to the vicar's unfortunately droning voice, which was reminiscent of a hive of agitated bees. I found myself drowsing. More than once a sharp elbow in the ribs from either Holmes or Lestrade brought me out of the start of a slumber. Both me shot me vaguely amused looks. After what seemed to be an interminably long time, the vicar finished speaking, the organist began playing, and we rose to take Thomas Arbuthnot to his final resting place.

The ladies were assisted back into their carriage to return home, and we followed the vicar to the graveside. More words were spoken as the coffin was lowered in. I found I was twisting my hat between my hands in some slight anguish. I have never dealt well with funerals. Having lost too many people I cared for in too short a time.

I found myself standing between David Catterick and Jenkins. Across the grave I could see Holmes and Lestrade standing on each side of Sir Lucas. Beyond them stood a knot of onlookers who had not been invited to the service. One of them was a tall man with a soft peaked cap pulled down shielding his face and wearing a scarf against the chill. For some reason he seemed vaguely familiar. Then the knot of people shifted and he disappeared from my view.

Our duties as pall-bearers completed, we adjourned with the others to have a quiet drink at one of the local pubs.

Lestrade took a sip of his pint and looked at Holmes. "Did you spot anyone interesting?" he asked.

Holmes shook his head.

I mentioned the man I had seen.

Holmes gave me an intent look. "He seemed familiar?"

I nodded. "But it could be something as simple as being someone I pass regularly in the street."

"It is possible, but unlikely," Holmes said. "Kensal Green is not on your regular round of places. I suggest, however, that you try to keep a hold of him in your memory. It may prove to be useful."

Holmes' expression was sour. "It is a pity that I was not standing on the opposite side of the grave. As it was I was situated in such a position that I would have had to turn my head to view the gawkers, and that, I am afraid, would have been a trifle too obvious."

My lips twitched into a slight smile. "That rather vocal vicar would probably have thrown his Bible at you."

"More likely a lump of sod from the grave," said Lestrade. "Bibles are expensive and vicars are usually impecunious."

Holmes took another sip of his beer, sighed, and then placed the glass down upon the table. "Have we finished here, gentlemen?"

Lestrade drained his pint. "Here, certainly, but we do need to return to the house and take our leave of the ladies."

I glanced about me, noting that Jenkins had already left. The man had drunk a half pint of beer, seeming very uncomfortable to be drinking with his master. I had formed the opinion that we were only having a drink here so that anyone who had not been invited to the funeral could come and say their condolences to Sir Lucas. No one came.

I looked around a little more carefully, seeking the man from the graveyard, but he had not joined our small company.

We strolled over to join Sir Lucas and his brother. Both men had finished their drinks and, like us, were preparing to leave.

The five of us returned to the house, where Jenkins was once again clad in his butler's uniform, happy to be back in his accustomed role.

A repast of sandwiches, cakes, and tea had been set out in the formal dining room. The parlour being off limits until it could be cleaned up from Arbuthnot's body lying there. It would take a while, too, for the memories of the coffin being centre stage in that room to fade from Sir Lucas' mind. Indeed, from the minds of all in the household.

I noticed that Lady Caroline was not present. Lady Amelia saw me looking around, and guessed for whom I was looking. "Mother has gone back up to bed," she said. "The poor dear found today both distressing and exhausting. She tended to view Thomas as part of the family. As did we all."

I nodded my understanding. It must be very difficult, I reflected, to go through life knowing you are different from other people. Not by choice, but by your very nature.

Lady Amelia introduced me to a charming lady with sparkling blue eyes. This was David's wife Rachel. Two blonde haired, blue-eyed cherubs peeked at me from behind her chair. These were David's sons and the reason Sir Lucas did not need to worry about the title.

I saw Holmes and Lestrade standing with Sir Lucas near the door, and walked with Lady Amelia towards them. Holmes barely concealed his impatience as I slipped upstairs to take my leave from Lady Caroline.

The old lady was sound asleep. I checked her pulse to make sure she was all right, but the pulse was firm and strong. Obviously the unaccustomed stress of the day had worn her out.

I came back downstairs to join my friends. We took a gracious farewell from our host and his family and walked out into the afternoon air.

We hailed a cab after a short walk, and sat in companionable silence as we headed back to Baker Street. We took our leave of Lestrade, who took the cab on to Scotland Yard.

Upstairs in our rooms, Holmes shed his hat and coat and threw himself into his chair with a deep sigh. "Well, my dear Watson, that was a complete waste of my time."

I went to demur, but he held up a hand to stop me.

"Yes, I know that it broadcast Sir Lucas' intentions. But in terms of actually furthering the investigation it was a complete waste of my time and energy."

I had to agree with him, and nodded reluctantly as I sat in my chair, reaching for the papers I had not had a chance to read properly that morning. Holmes stuffed his pipe with tobacco and soon the room was filled with aromatic smoke that was almost as thick as a London fog. I sighed, and got up to open a window. Holmes' response was to refill his pipe and continue smoking. .

Mrs. Hudson complained bitterly when she brought up our evening meal. Holmes ignored her, whilst I attempted to apologize. She patted me on the arm as she left. "Never mind, dear, we both know what he gets like when he gets in one of these moods." The look Mrs. Hudson shot Holmes had daggers in it.

I hid a smile and turned my attention to the sausages, mash, and peas that had been provided for us.

Once we had dined we returned to our usual seats and waited for Mrs. Hudson to return to clear the table before we talked about the case again.

Holmes was scraping tunelessly on his violin, leading me to think that an evening walk would be an excellent idea, despite the growing coldness of the night.

Downstairs someone banged hard upon the door. I heard Mrs. Hudson open it, then a young, agitated, voice, followed by Mrs. Hudson calling out in a cross tone, as someone ran up the stairs.

Holmes put his violin down and leaned forward just as the door flew open. One of the Baker Street Irregulars stood there, panting for breath. It was young Timothy, a recent member of the Irregulars and one of their swiftest runners.

"Wiggins sent me, Mr. 'Olmes," the boy said. "Some bugger's set the 'ouse in Cleveland Street on fire!"

We both leaped to our feet, grabbing for our coats, hats, and, in deference to the growing chill, our scarves.

I noticed Timothy eying the remains of our meal that still stood upon the table. Without saying a word, Holmes grabbed a slice of bread and wrapped it around an untouched sausage and handed it to the lad.

The boy had good manners. At least, I assume the words I heard from him were "thank you," muffled as they were by the bread and sausage jammed in his mouth.

We ran down the stairs, past Mrs. Hudson standing by the front door, who glared at us as we shot past, Timothy on our heels.

"No point in hailing a cab, Watson," said Holmes. "The police will never let a cab get close to the scene."

So we set off at a brisk pace in the direction of Cleveland Street, Timothy darting ahead of us, no doubt in search of Wiggins.

By the time we reached Cleveland Street the London Fire Brigade had arrived and were working on dousing the flames that could be seen through the open front door of the house. Uniformed police constables were keeping the gathering crowd of curious bystanders at bay.

I turned to an elderly gentleman leaning on a walking stick who stood next to me. "Do you know what happened?" Things like a fire tended to make Londoners more inclined to talk to strangers. After all, what is the point of having news if you cannot share it?

The elderly gent looked at me with sharp blue eyes. "No one is really sure. The lady who lived there and her companion shifted out a short while ago. The house was vacant. Probably some tramp found his way inside looking for a warm place to sleep and accidentally set fire to the house."

Holmes snorted rudely.

My informant gave him an indignant look. "I suppose you have a better suggestion, sir?"

Holmes ignored him. He was scanning the crowd.

A lithe figure wriggled between the masses and fetched up beside Holmes. It was Wiggins. He was short lad, built like a whippet, with mouse-brown hair, and hazel eyes that usually sparkled with both mischief and hero-worship for Holmes.

He grinned impudently up at Holmes. "Archie was watchin' the back and saw 'im go in. I saw 'im through the window moving about at the front. Then a few minutes later 'e slips out the front door and goes up the street towards Euston Road. Just after that I sees smoke. I sent Timmy to you, and sent Archie for the rozzers. Told 'im to tell 'em that it was for one of the Inspector's cases. I know some of them buggers don't like you much."

Holmes chuckled richly. "Well done, Wiggins." He slipped the lad some coins. Wiggins grinned at him again, signaled to Timothy and Archie, who was sliding through the crowd towards us.

"That young man is very resourceful. He will go far," I observed, watching the three young lads slip away into the night.

"That he will, Watson." Holmes' response had a slightly abstracted tone to it.

I looked around to see what had distracted my friend. Following his gaze I saw Lestrade had arrived at the other end of the cordon, and begun to converse with the uniformed sergeant who was obviously in charge.

My friend stood patiently, waiting for Lestrade to notice that we were here. It did not take him long. Lestrade turned away from his colleague, an irritated expression crossing his face, and saw us standing there. He said something to a young constable nearby, who came hurrying across to let us past.

Lestrade's irritated expression had morphed into one of annoyance by the time we reached his side.

"Did you know this was going to happen?" he demanded.

Holmes shook his head. "I asked the Irregulars to keep an eye on the house. I thought it possible that the killer could return, no doubt to try and discover where it was that Mrs. Swindon had gone, but I thought it unlikely. I did not suspect that he would attempt to burn the place to the ground."

"The man is insane!" I said.

"Quite possibly," said Holmes. "Sane people do not usually set things on fire!"

Lestrade looked around and sighed. "We were lucky. This could easily have turned into a conflagration. Though the sergeant tells me that he had no idea what he was doing."

"Oh?" Holmes gave Lestrade a look of curiosity.

"In most cases like this, the person would soak the curtains in paraffin and light them. Goes up like a torch. This idiot tried to build a fire in the middle of the hall floor. Not enough easily burnable material, because the floor is sheathed with marble tiles, so the fire brigade was able to extinguish it quickly enough. If he had soaked the curtains, we would probably have lost half of Marylebone."

Lestrade gave my friend a somewhat sour look. "How can we be dealing with someone who is clever enough to commit four murders and not get caught, but cannot even start a fire properly?"

"He is rattled," Holmes said softly. "He is beginning to make mistakes. Since killing Evelyn Smythe, he has not had a thing go right for him."

"Could he be upset at killing the wrong woman and that is knocking him off balance?" I asked.

"Upset at killing?" Lestrade snorted. "He had killed three people up to that point."

"Watson is correct," my friend said. "Yes, he had killed three people, but they appear to have been deliberate kills within a defined plan. Though I have my doubts about the killing of Bradstreet. Evelyn Smythe was mistaken identity. It had to unbalance him. Once he saw in the papers that he had killed an innocent widow, well, it is obvious that it has been playing on his mind."

"Playing on his mind," Lestrade repeated softly, understanding at last what Holmes and I meant.

Holmes nodded. "Sooner or later he will make a critical mistake, and we will get him. Make no mistake about that!"

"Did the young lad have any trouble getting to you?" I asked.

Lestrade chuckled. "He kicked up a right old stink when the sergeant on the public desk would not listen to him. Kept yelling my name. Sergeant was about to boot his arse out into the street when I came through the front. Knew at once it was one of Holmes' urchins. Also knew he would not be there to waste my time."

"He went all the way to Scotland Yard?" Holmes was startled.

Lestrade nodded. "He grabbed a constable on the street before then and told him about the fire. That officer at least had the good sense to listen to him." Lestrade grinned widely. "The constable is also resourceful and quick thinking. I am tracking down his name and getting him transferred to the Yard."

"Why?" I asked.

Lestrade's grin grew even wider. "When the boy told him the details, the constable flagged down a cab, stuck the lad in it, paid the cabbie, and told him to drive like hell for Scotland Yard. I brought the lad back with me. He can certainly talk though. Asked me all about being a policeman. I think he wants to be one. Pity he cannot read."

The look upon Holmes' face was one of sheer delight. "That can be fixed. Even if I have to teach him to read myself."

I could not hold back a snort of amusement. "You do not have the temperament to be a teacher, Holmes. You are not the most patient of people after all. Besides, what are you going to use as school books? Your scrapbooks of lurid and sensational crime?

"I thought I might use back issues of the Strand Magazine. After all, they do print a lot of childish drivel."

Lestrade smiled tiredly. "I do not think there is much else that can be done tonight. We cannot go into the building yet. If you gentlemen would like to join me here at 10 o'clock tomorrow morning, we might be able to have a look inside then. I shall leave several constables on duty overnight. That should stop our maniac returning, and also comfort the locals whom I heard grumbling about the possibility of being burned alive in their beds as I arrived."

Holmes nodded. "A sound idea, Lestrade. We bid you a good night, and we shall see you in the morning."

It was dark and cold, and this time we hailed a cab to take us back to Baker Street.

Upon our return, I built up the fire to take the chill off our hastily abandoned rooms. I noted that Mrs. Hudson had cleared away the detritus of our meal. Holmes poured us both a brandy and we settled in comfortably before the flames.

I watched the flames dance for a while, aware that Holmes was brooding and somewhat restless in his chair.

I looked across at him. He was staring into the fireplace, a morose expression on his face. Aware of my scrutiny, he looked up and gave me the smallest of smiles.

"Do you think we will catch him, Holmes?" I asked.

"We have to, Watson. He is now extremely unbalanced and even more dangerous than he was previously. And I am very much afraid that he will kill again before we do."

"Maybe we will get to him before that."

Holmes heaved a sigh. "I doubt that, my friend. I truly doubt it."

Chapter Ten

The next morning found us waiting for Lestrade outside the fire-damaged house in Cleveland Street. He arrived precisely at ten and we walked silently up the steps.

The door hung open, swaying slightly in the morning breeze. Pools of water lay on the floor, and the smell of acrid smoke lay heavily in the air. The damage, however, was relatively minor. Several marble floor tiles were cracked and stained from the heat, scorch marks up a wall, charcoal and ash on the floor where the fire was started, and, everywhere, a pervading layer of soot.

Holmes looked around briefly, a small frown on his face. "I am uncertain that there is much to be learned from this. As you said last night, Lestrade, this was an extremely clumsy attempt to burn the place down. I do wonder if our man even knows how to start a fire, except in a fireplace or stove."

"What do you mean?" I asked.

Holmes gestured at the floor. "Look at it, Watson. He has piled small sticks upon the floor as kindling. And, judging by the smell, has used a small plug of paraffin wax as a fire starter." Holmes snorted his contempt. "He has not realized that for a fire like this to work it needs a flue to create airflow and drive the fire. Opening the door created some airflow, but it was too early. The amount of air coming in could as easily have extinguished the flame as allow it to burn freely. The only reason the fire took was because a spark caught the drapery hanging off that small table against the wall."

He gestured to where the scorch mark seared up the wall, and where a pile of burned and scorched wood sat jumbled in an untidy heap upon the floor. I realized that the pile of debris had been a small table similar to one which sat in Mrs. Hudson's hallway.

Holmes frowned. "We know our man is young, given his speed and general athleticism. It appears that he also lives alone. His hours are too erratic for him to be married. Most married men are men of routine. Work, clubs, home. Wives expect it of them. His inability to properly start a fire also suggests that he either lives in fully serviced rooms, or in a room, possibly over his place of business, where he only has a small stove for warmth. I suspect the later. Landladies are quite nearly as inquisitive as wives are, and are often even less understanding."

"Then we are finished here?" asked Lestrade.

Holmes nodded. "I doubt there is anything else to be learned from this bungled attempt at arson."

We left the house, and, taking our leave from Lestrade, returned to Baker Street.

I sat down and began to write up my notes on the case, taking care to include Holmes' observations on the likely domestic arrangements of our killer. The more I thought about it, the more sense it made. The killings had garnered a lot of interest in the newspapers, even if they had not been linked into a pattern by the reporters, the way Holmes had linked them together. If the killer were living with someone, by now, surely, that person would have come forward with suspicions. After all, there are only so many times a person can return home with his clothes spotted with blood before even the most obtuse of persons would begin to realize something was amiss.

It was hard for me to concentrate, as Holmes was prowling the room like a caged tiger. He stopped at the window and stared down into the street.

I looked up from my writing. "Something interesting, Holmes?"

"We are about to have visitors, Watson."

I put my pen down and closed my notebook. "Anyone interesting?"

"Mrs. Gertrude Swindon and Miss Dorothy Watts," he replied.

I smiled to myself at how quickly we had both begun to refer to the lad, named Daniel by his parents, as Dorothy, and the equal speed with which we had both accepted that he was truly a she and entitled to the preferred name of Dorothy. It occurred to me I had no idea what Lestrade thought of Dorothy. I hoped he would end up being as accepting as Holmes and I.

"You are possibly expecting too much of Lestrade, Watson," Holmes observed. "The great institution that is the London Metropolitan Police is somewhat rigid in its attitudes towards what it perceives to be right and normal."

"Really, Holmes, That is too much! You should be on the stage at a music hall: Sherlock Holmes the Magnificent, Reader of Minds."

Holmes smiled lightly. "There is not much to read amongst the musical hall crowd, my friend. It really was a straightforward observation."

"Oh? I fail to see how knew that I was thinking about Lestrade's attitude to Dorothy."

Holmes gestured at my notebook. "The last thing you wrote before setting down your pen was about Lestrade's observations on the fire. When I mentioned the arrival of our visitors, you looked down at your notebook at my mention of Dorothy's name, and you frowned slightly. Then you touched your shoulder briefly. You only touch your shoulder in that manner when you are thinking of Afghanistan. The only reason you had for doing that was a fleeting remembrance of the female soldier you told me about. Perhaps a momentary thought on how the military hierarchy would have reacted to that soldier, had they known what you discovered. It was but a short step to link that thought to Lestrade."

"Several hundred years ago, Mr. Holmes, you would have burned at the stake as a witch."

We both looked towards the doorway, where our visitors now stood. It was Gertrude who had made the observation. She smiled at us both.

Holmes ushered our guests to chairs, as he commented, "Only in Scotland, ma'am. In England most witches were hanged."

We both sat in our accustomed seats.

"You have been to the house, I see," said Holmes.

Even I could smell the faint, sour, smell of smoke that lingered about the ladies. No doubt Holmes and I smelled the vaguely similar odor.

"Indeed," replied Gertrude. "I needed to see the extent of the damage and if it would be repairable. Thankfully, there was little damage and all easily fixed. A few new floor tiles, new wallpaper and a lick of paint will see it right."

Dorothy leaned forward. "We need to talk to you, Mr. Holmes. Every time we go out, we are being followed."

"Followed?" I asked.

Gertrude nodded. "We first noticed it the day before Thomas' funeral. Every time Dorothy or I go out, a young lad follows us. Not always the same one, mind you."

"They stand out," Dorothy said, "because they do not quite fit in."

Holmes raised his eyebrows in query and gestured for her to continue.

"They are not local boys. We are used to those hanging around looking at the house where the man who was murdered lived. These lads, whilst clean and in suitable clothes for the area, do not seem to know Kensington at all well."

"They do not," Holmes said with a vaguely rueful expression.

"You know who they are?" asked Gertrude.

Holmes nodded. "They are some of my Irregulars. I had them cleaned up, suitably clothed, and lodged with an acquaintance of mine who lives quite close to Sir Lucas' house. They are keeping watch on you and, particularly, on anyone who takes an interest in you. There is a system in place to report to me if they spot anything amiss. Their leader, Wiggins, is coordinating the effort. Archie is in charge at Kensington, with two or three others assisting him. The rest of the lads are keeping an eye on the places where the murders occurred. Just in case the killer decides to return."

"Archie would be the one with blonde curls and blue eyes? Looks rather like a Botticelli cherub? Quick witted as well?" asked Dorothy.

"That does indeed sound like Archie," Holmes agreed. "Though there is very little cherubic about the lad, he does have a good heart."

Dorothy smiled. "When we were leaving this morning he realized that we had spotted him, So he came sauntering towards us, raised his cap and wished us a good morning, before carrying on around the corner. I noticed he stowed away on the back of the carriage as we left."

I burst out laughing. "Quick-witted indeed. He was the lad who raised the alarm at Cleveland Street. He made the acquaintance of Inspector Lestrade last night and now wants to be a policeman."

"He is a dedicated lad," said Holmes. "Once he was certain that both of you were safely inside for the night, he joined Wiggins at Cleveland Street. Archie is observant. By now he has worked out exactly what is and is not acceptable in a house in mourning and is tailoring his movements accordingly."

Gertrude got to her feet and Dorothy followed suit. "I am glad we do not need to worry then, Mr. Holmes. Are you getting any nearer to catching this man?"

Holmes shook his head. "We still have no idea as to his identity. However, he is rattled and beginning to make mistakes. Rest assured that we will get him."

"I believe that you will," Gertrude replied.

Both ladies swept out of the room, closing the door softly behind them.

Our next visitor, about half an hour later, was not quite so pleasant a diversion, as the ponderous tread upon our stairs signaled the arrival of Mycroft Holmes.

He lowered himself into one of our chairs with a sigh. "Sherlock, Doctor Watson."

"What brings you here, Mycroft? At this time of the day you should be firmly ensconced in your office in Whitehall."

Mycroft settled himself more comfortably in the chair. "Certain people wish to know what progress you have made in finding the murderer." He did not enlighten us as to whom these people were.

"The killer is as intangible as the Whitechapel killer ever was. I am no stage magician to pluck a murderous rabbit from a top hat," Holmes said sharply.

"We have a lot of information," I added hurriedly, before the discussion could descend to the level of a family squabble. "We just do not have the pieces necessary to link the information together."

Mycroft hummed thoughtfully.

Holmes was staring out the window. "The killer is getting bolder. Evelyn Smythe was murdered just off the Strand in the early evening."

"Evelyn Smythe?" Mycroft asked.

Holmes swung around to glare at him. "Do you not read the newspapers?"

"Of course, but the connection…?"

"The connection," Holmes snapped, "…is one of mistaken identity. The victim bore an uncanny resemble to Gertrude Swindon."

Mycroft Holmes got the point immediately. "The killer thought he had killed Gertrude Swindon, and now he is going to pieces having killed an innocent."

"More than that," I said with a sad shake of my head. "Mrs. Smythe was a widow. She left four children. A girl in service, a son working as a telegraph boy, and two young ones who are now most probably hungry and terrified in a workhouse, as Lestrade told us there were no relatives."

Mycroft gazed at me for a moment. I stared back coldly, defying him to make a comment as to my tender-heartedness. He made no comment, but turned back to his brother.

"What are you planning to do now?"

"I do believe that Watson and I need to take to the streets."

I raised my eyebrows in query.

"Perambulations of the Strand, and perhaps the Embankment. Those are the areas that seem to be his major hunting ground. It is unlikely that we will catch him, but perhaps we may encounter a possible witness or two, at the very least we will have had some pleasant exercise."

"That smacks of desperation, Sherlock," Mycroft observed.

"We are desperate, Mycroft. All that I have are loose threads and odd patches of cloth that I cannot even begin to weave into a logical garment."

Mycroft nodded. "Do you need an assistance? I can detail some of my employees to assist."

"Thank you for the offer, Mycroft, but no. If they are as useful as Jeremiah Bradstreet was, I doubt they could succeed in finding a wandering pie-man, let alone a deranged killer."

"Holmes!" I glared at him, then turned to Mycroft. "Give us a week by ourselves. If we have no success, then we will accept your offer with gratitude."

Mycroft gave me a ghost of a smile. "Not with gratitude, I think."

Mycroft rose from his seat, wished us both a good day, and departed, no doubt back to his office in Whitehall.

Holmes stood at the window, watching him go, then he turned back towards me, a frown creasing his brows.

"It seems I have committed you to at least a week of wandering London in all weathers. I apologize, my friend."

I shrugged. "We need to catch him. I admit that I will not rest easily until this monster is caught. He is dangerous."

"He is that," Holmes agreed. "What say we take dinner at Simpson's again this evening? To fortify ourselves against the weather."

"That sounds like an excellent idea to me," I said.

I turned back to my notes on the case, and Holmes wandered across to his desk; I heard him take his violin out of its case. A flicker of irritation crossed my face. I really wanted to concentrate on my notes, but if Holmes tortured his violin, that would be impossible. However, Holmes must have sensed my mood as the soft strains of Bach filled the room, and I returned to my writing.

Chapter Eleven

We had no success that evening nor the following one. It was the evening after that that all the threads began to weave together into a rather horrific finale.

We were close to the site of Evelyn Smythe's murder, when we began to hear a commotion ahead of us. Exchanging a look, we increased our stride towards the noise. A small figure came barreling down the road towards us. It was young Archie from the Irregulars.

He grabbed the edge of Holmes' coat. "Come quick, Mr. 'Olmes. There's bin another an' Miss Dorothy an' me seen it."

"Dorothy? What on earth is she doing here?" I asked in shock.

Archie looked up at me. "She's bin tryin' to get the 'hores off the street. Came down 'ere to talk to Daisy. We walked around the corner and saw this cove choking Daisy. 'E seen us an' ran away."

"You were with her?" Holmes asked, almost as shocked as I was.

Archie grinned. "Miss Dorothy came to me outside the 'ouse an' said if I was gonna watch over 'er, then I'd best do it in comfort." The grin got broader and filled with pride. "I bin ridin' in the carriage with 'er when she goes out."

From the look on Holmes' face it was clear he was unsure whether to laugh at the revelation or not. I hid a smile.

"You left Miss Dorothy alone?" Holmes asked.

Archie shook his head. "Nope. Wiggins is with 'er. 'E was close, an' heard the racket. Said for me to go run an' fetch you."

Holmes looked at me. "Time we joined them, do you not think, Watson?"

"Most definitely, Holmes."

With Archie scurrying to keep up with us, we strode along the Strand.

We arrived into the middle of a most dreadful scene. A uniformed police constable was yelling at Dorothy, calling her a whore and other vile and filthy names.

Holmes' face lit with anger and he began to stride towards the constable, just as the man drew has arm back and slapped Dorothy hard across the face.

With a roar of adolescent fury, Archie streaked across the intervening ground and kicked the constable hard in the shins. "Bastard mutton shunter!" the boy yelled indignantly. "Treatin' a lady like that!"

The man swatted at Archie and turned back, arm raised to strike Dorothy again, and found someone else in her place.

He looked into the furious, dark blue, eyes of Inspector Lestrade, who had just arrived on the scene. Before the man could say a word, Lestrade's fist lashed out. There was a sickening crunch of bone and cartilage, as the constable's nose broke, and he staggered backward and fell onto the street under the force of the blow.

Lestrade stood over him, eyes blazing, his voice colder and more angry than I had ever heard from the little detective before. "A fine way to treat a woman and a witness. You are a disgrace to the uniform. Sergeant?"

He never took his eyes from the cowering constable, whose nose was streaming blood onto his uniform tunic. Contempt for the man showed in every line of Lestrade's body.

The sergeant we had met at Evelyn Smythe's murder came across, a barely concealed grin on his face. "Yes, Inspector?"

"Get this man out of here. I do not want to see him again outside of a disciplinary hearing."

"Right you are, sir." He signaled to a couple of other constables who dragged the man away. Their rough handling of him suggested that the man was not popular with his fellow policemen.

The crowd, who had fallen silent at the spectacle, began to whoop and cheer. Whistling their approval of Lestrade's actions.

Startled, Lestrade's head whipped around and he stared at them in something akin to shock. It was clear he had been so focused on rescuing Dorothy that he had not registered the presence of a large crowd of bystanders. Londoners, as a mob, do not usually care for policemen. In recent years officers of the law had been viewed as officers of oppression. But at this moment, Lestrade was the hero of the London mob. He blushed a deep red as the more forward female members of the crowd blew him kisses.

Holmes hid a smile. "I stand corrected, my dear Watson. You did not expect too much of Lestrade. I expected too little of him. In fact the good inspector has well surpassed both of our expectations. I suspect that we had best rescue him, however, before he demonstrates whether or not it is possible to die of mortification."

Lestrade did indeed look deeply embarrassed by the adulation the mob was giving him. He looked relieved to see both of us. Not his usual expression upon seeing us at one of his crime scenes.

He was flexing his right hand as we came up to him. I frowned at him. "Really Lestrade, you should not go around punching people like that. You could have broken your hand."

Lestrade looked at me for a long moment, then gave a shaky laugh. "Never mind my hand. I think I broke the brute's nose."

"You did," Holmes confirmed. "I heard the crunch from where Watson and I were standing." He gave Lestrade a mischievous look. "A good solid blow, but your technique needs a little work. Once this case is completed I would be delighted to assist you with that."

Lestrade looked to me for an explanation.

"Bare-knuckle fighter," I said.

Lestrade shook his head in admiration. "Is there anything you cannot do, Mr. Holmes?"

As the question was obviously rhetorical, I ignored it in favour of examining Lestrade's hand. To my relief the hand was not broken, but the knuckles were badly bruised and the skin split in a couple of places. I clucked my tongue in annoyance.

The light fragrance of lavender wafted around me, and Dorothy silently handed me a black silk kerchief. I thanked her with a brief smile, and carefully bound Lestrade's hand.

"There," said Holmes drily. "Now that Lestrade's wounds of honour have been attended to, perhaps we may attend to the crime."

I looked around for Dorothy. She had moved away to stand near the mouth of a lane way, with Archie hovering protectively at her side. Wiggins leaned against a wall nearby. He was frowning in the direction that the abusive constable had been dragged.

The sergeant had obtained a damp cloth from somewhere and had proffered it to Dorothy, who held it against her cheek.

The three of us went to join them, and the sergeant directed our attention up the lane way to where a corpse in female clothing lay in a huddled mass on the cobblestones. Lestrade and Holmes headed up the lane. I paused beside Dorothy to inspect her injury. To my intense relief the brute of a constable had not hit hard enough to break bone, but her face would be bruised for days.

As I turned to go and join Holmes and Lestrade, Dorothy laid her hand upon my arm. "I need to talk to Mr. Holmes and Inspector Lestrade, Doctor Watson. I got a good look at the killer."

"I will bring them back here as soon as they have examined the corpse," I promised. As I headed up the alley, I turned and looked back, as a thought struck me. "Did you recognize the victim?"

Dorothy nodded. "She used the name Daisy. Used to live at Cleveland Street but, like Nancy, went back to the streets full time. She was only fifteen."

I nodded my thanks and hurried to join my companions.

Holmes was crouched beside the body, magnifying glass in hand. "He did not have the time to complete his ritual, Dorothy and Archie's arrival saw to that."

"How did she die?" I asked.

Lestrade pointed to the red marks on the throat. "Strangled." He gave a half smile. "Even a humble Scotland Yard detective can work that out without assistance."

Holmes snorted. "Our killer did not quite manage to take this one unawares. She fought back. Possibly he could not get his hand over her mouth. Oh!" He leaned forward and peered at her mouth. Then he grinned delightedly. "Good lass! She bit him! Look closely, you can see blood on her teeth and lips."

Taking the glass from Holmes I looked carefully at the mouth of the corpse. Sure enough, a little blood flecked the lips and teeth. A quick check showed she had not bitten her tongue or the inside of her mouth, so the blood must be from her killer.

I handed the glass to Lestrade, who had a brief look and nodded his agreement.

"Is it too much to ask he gets rabies?" Lestrade asked sourly.

"Sepsis is more likely," I replied. "Especially if he cannot keep the wound clean."

"Well, if nothing else, it would at least save the government the cost of a trial and subsequent execution," said Holmes, continuing his examination.

Lestrade stared at the corpse morosely. "I have the nasty feeling that when we catch this one, he is going to end up in either Colney Hatch or Broadmoor, rather than morrising at the end of a rope."

Holmes looked up at Lestrade, then back down at the corpse. "I sincerely hope not. I do not usually say this, but there are some crimes where the killer truly deserves to die. This is one of them. Indeed he deserves to hang for the death of Evelyn Smythe alone."

"And for the fate to which he has condemned her children," I added.

Lestrade looked sideways at us both, but forbore to speak.

Holmes switched his attention to the hands of the victim. He gave an exultant cry, leaning forward to gently uncurl a small closed fist. Lestrade and I glimpsed a flash of something small and gold, before it disappeared into Holmes' pocket.

"That is evidence, Holmes," Lestrade said tartly. "It is rightfully the property of Scotland Yard."

"All in good time, my dear Lestrade." Holmes turned a grin that was almost maniacal on both of us. "There is someone I want to show it to first." He got easily to his feet.

The grin made me suspicious. "You know who the killer is? Don't you?"

"You remember my comment about having an absurd theory?"

"After we had visited Mrs. Bradstreet?" I asked, casting my mind back to that day.

"Let us just say that my theory has just become a little less absurd," said Holmes. "Though the motive is still unknown, I am beginning to have some distinct suspicions upon that score as well."

Lestrade looked down at the corpse. I do not suppose we know who this victim is?"

"Dorothy says her name was Daisy. She was a former resident of Cleveland Street." I looked down at the corpse as well, and sighed. "According to Dorothy, she was only fifteen. Oh, and Dorothy wants a word with us when you have finished."

"Have you finished, Holmes?" asked Lestrade.

Holmes nodded. "I do not believe it is necessary to attend the morgue this time."

He ignored the shudder of relief that went through me. I may be used to death as a doctor, but that does not mean that I welcome time spent close to its embrace.

"I think there is more to be learned from Dorothy, and young Archie, than there is from poor Daisy's remains," Holmes added.

Lestrade signaled to the sergeant to begin removal of the body, and we walked back up to the Strand where Dorothy and Archie were waiting.

"Miss Dorothy," Holmes greeted her cordially.

"Mr. Holmes," she replied.

Dorothy then flashed a shy smile at Lestrade. "Thank you for your rescue, Inspector."

Lestrade doffed his hat. He looked more than a little embarrassed again. "You are welcome, Miss. Men like that constable have no business being in the police. Give every officer a bad name."

Holmes intervened smoothly, before Lestrade could get any more flustered. "Watson tells me that you knew the victim?"

Dorothy nodded. "She was known as Daisy. I know her family named her James, and that she was fifteen. Gertrude will probably have the rest of the details."

"We will speak with Mrs. Swindon when we see you safely home," Lestrade said.

"I understand from my good Watson that you and young Archie saw the killer," said Holmes.

"We seen 'im, alright," Archie butted in. "A right rum cove that one. 'E was wearing a dress."

"A dress?" I blinked in astonishment.

Lestrade's mouth gaped slightly. "You mean he was a she?"

Dorothy shook her head firmly. "No. It was a man dressed as a woman, but not a man who is truly a woman. He looked and moved wrong."

Holmes considered that for a moment, before saying, "By that I take it that you mean he was obviously uncomfortable in the dress."

"Yeah," said Archie. "'E was wriggling around like a worm on an 'ook. An' when 'e ran for it, 'e 'itched 'is skirt up! Not even the cheapest 'ore in the Chapel would 'oik 'er skirts up like that."

"The Chapel?" I murmured to Lestrade.

"Whitechapel," he murmured back.

"There is something else," Dorothy said softly. "I recognized him."

All three of us stared at her.

She looked at the three of us, her expression troubled. "But I do not know how I could."

"Why is that?" Lestrade asked gently.

"Because the man he looked like is dead. Mickey is dead. He was a client of both Molly and Nancy. He jumped from Westminster Bridge several months ago. Molly cried about it for days."

In all the years that I have known my friend, I have never once failed to be impressed with the speed at which his brain works. Within seconds I could see understanding bloom on his face. "Mickey. Michael. Michael Croft!"

Holmes looked at Dorothy and Archie. "The dress he was wearing. Was it perchance silk damask in spring green with gold lace cuffs and collar?"

Dorothy put her hand to her mouth to cover her surprise. "Why yes, Mr. Holmes. How did you know?"

Holmes put his hand in his pocket and withdrew the item he had taken from Daisy's hand. He opened his hand to reveal an intricate gold button attached to a scrap of gold lace. It looked very like it should belong to the dress that Viola Bradstreet had described to us.

Realization dawned on me at much the same time that it did on Lestrade.

"The killer is Nathaniel?" My voice held shock and disbelief.

Holmes gave me a bitter smile. "If you remember I did muse as to why he shaved off his moustache."

"Michael Croft's twin," said Lestrade. "Identical twin, obviously. But why?"

"Watson can tell you that," said Holmes. "He was the one who found it."

"I did?" I asked.

"In the post-mortem report," Holmes replied.

I thought for a moment. "The report was fairly straight forward. Nothing that you would not expect from a possible suicide, except... Oh!" I blushed faintly and tried not to look at Dorothy or Archie.

Holmes took pity on me. He looked at Lestrade, "Michael Croft was also suffering from the start of a very nasty ailment that often affects men who consort with..." Holmes paused, also not wanting to be crude in front of Dorothy.

"You mean 'e had the pox, don'tcha, Mr. 'Olmes?" said Archie.

"Out of the mouths of babes," muttered Lestrade, who was struggling to keep a straight face at the expressions on both mine and Holmes' faces.

Dorothy turned away to hide her smile at our mutual discomfort.

Lestrade signaled to the sergeant who came to join us.

"Yes, inspector?"

"The lady and the lad both saw the killer. We now think we know who he is, but it will take a while to track down where he is living and arrange an arresting party."

"That is good news, sir."

"Meanwhile, we need to keep our two witnesses safe. The lady will be safe at her home amongst family retainers, but I am reluctant to have both our witnesses in the same place."

"I can understand that, sir." The sergeant gave Archie a speculative look. "You're the lad who wants to be a copper now, aren't you? How would you like to come and stay with me and my missus for a time? We'll keep you safe and feed you, and you can come to the station with me and see what a policeman's job is really like."

Archie's eyes lit up. He looked at Holmes. "Can I, Mr. 'Olmes?"

Holmes could not forbear smiling at Archie's enthusiasm. "I believe that to be an excellent idea, Archie."

"We'll keep a close eye on him, Mr. Holmes. The missus will be pleased to have another lad to care for, after our eldest moved out a few months back. And don't worry, I'll keep him away from Watkins. That bastard won't get a chance to get his own back for his kicked shins."

"Watkins?" Lestrade frowned. "He is the one who keeps skiving off duty?"

"Yes, sir. Reckon this time he'll be out on his arse. Pardon my language, miss." The sergeant bobbed a little bow to Dorothy.

Holmes slipped a couple of sovereigns to the sergeant, and murmured something to him, which the sergeant replied to equally softly. The sergeant then placed his hand on Archie's shoulder and led him away, so the lad could watch as the corpse was removed and the scene cleared.

Wiggins pushed himself off the wall he had been leaning on and joined us.

"I've seen 'im before," Wiggins said.

"The sergeant?" I asked.

"No. That bloody constable. Watkins. 'E was hanging around Cleveland Street when the 'ouse was burnin'."

"Was he now?" Holmes said softly. He looked at Lestrade. "I do believe we need to find out just what circumstances link Constable Watkins with Nathaniel Croft."

"Whatever it is, we will find it," Lestrade assured him.

Holmes nodded and turned back to Wiggins. "Thank you, Wiggins. You have confirmed something I was beginning to suspect." He slipped the lad a few coins and the boy disappeared into the rapidly thinning crowd.

We walked with Dorothy to where Sir Lucas' coachman was waiting with the carriage. The man's bored expression turned to one of shock when he saw Dorothy's face.

Lestrade handed Dorothy up into the carriage, and the three of us then joined her.

We rode in silence back to Sir Lucas' Kensington house.

Upon our arrival, Jenkins took one look at Dorothy and sent a footman to fetch Sir Lucas, Lady Amelia, and Gertrude Swindon, before seating us all in the parlour and hurrying away to arrange for tea to be supplied. Tea is an Englishman's response to almost any crisis.

Gertrude arrived first. She took one look at Dorothy's face and let out a sharp cry. "What happened?"

"A brutal bully of a policeman is what happened," Lestrade said grimly. "And I can tell you now that if I have my way he will not be a policeman for much longer."

Sir Lucas, entering the room with his mother, heard Lestrade's comment. "What is this man's name?"

"Constable Watkins. Based out of A division," Lestrade replied.

Lady Amelia seated herself and asked "What actually happened?"

"Dorothy and Archie walked into the middle of a murder," I said.

"Where is Archie?" Gertrude asked, looking up from where she was examining Dorothy's face.

"With two witnesses to a murder, ma'am, we thought it best to keep them separate to keep them safe. Archie is staying with Sergeant Halliday from A Division and his wife. Archie's about the age of their eldest boy who went to the bad," Lestrade replied.

At my querying expression, Lestrade explained, "He got caught thieving. The lad's currently in Reading Gaol. Halliday and his wife took it hard."

"That does not surprise me," Holmes said softly.

"Who was the victim?" asked Gertrude.

"It was Daisy," replied Dorothy.

Gertrude sighed. "One of my failures. I still had hopes for Molly when she was killed. That I could get her off the streets properly, not just when she felt like it. But Daisy was completely wild."

"Did Daisy have family?" Lestrade asked. "We will need to contact them."

"Daisy was born James Macklin," Gertrude replied. "While still trying to be male, he worked as a telegraph boy. He was fired for misconduct about six months ago. Nancy took him under her wing. Showed him how to be female. That is when she took the name Daisy. When Nancy was killed, Molly started to watch over her. Dorothy and I had been trying to get Daisy off the streets for the last three months. With a distinct lack of success, I might add."

"The telegraph office should still have the details we need. There will be no need to tell any family the full circumstances of Daisy's death."

"You are a good man, Inspector Lestrade," Gertrude said warmly.

Lestrade's ears went faintly pink.

Scenting blood, my friend said, with just a hint of mischief in his tone, "This evening he broke the nose of the policeman who hit Dorothy. It was as fine a display of gallantry as ever a novelist created. All fire and fury. It was rather like a medieval tournament. The lady even supplying her favour to bandage his wounds." Holmes gestured towards Lestrade's hand where the black silk kerchief was bound around his knuckles.

Lestrade glared at Holmes.

I laughed. "You are a fine one to talk, Holmes. You were steaming up the Strand in a rare fury. If Lestrade had not got there first, it would have been you breaking Watkins' nose for him." I chuckled. "As it was, young Archie nearly broke his shins for him. That was quite a kicking he administered."

Dorothy suddenly looked anxious. "That constable will not be able to hurt Archie, will he? With him staying at with the sergeant from the same division?"

"Not a chance," Lestrade said. "Halliday does not like Watkins and was, I suspect, amused by Archie's attack. He will keep the lad safe."

"Given the reactions of the other constables," Holmes observed, "I do not believe that anyone much cares for Watkins."

"He does not pull his weight on his shifts and continually skives off," Lestrade said. "No one likes someone who creates work for others through sheer laziness."

After a few more pleasantries and reassurances, we took our leave of the household. Sir Lucas insisting on his coachman taking us back to our respective rooms.

Chapter Twelve

I woke reasonably early the next morning and wandered out to partake of breakfast. After about fifteen minutes, Holmes joined me. Helping himself to eggs and devilled kidneys, he joined me in a silent communion of appreciation of Mrs. Hudson's culinary talents.

Whilst we were breakfasting a messenger arrived from Mycroft with instructions to attend on him at his office in Whitehall.

We finished our morning coffee before hastening out onto Baker Street and hailing a cab. The streets were thick with a sulphurous yellow fog that tore at the throat and made the eyes water.

Mycroft's office was tucked away in an older building that nestled in the shadow of the ancient edifice that is Westminster Abbey. He was seated behind a sturdy desk made of polished oak, reading over some papers; he looked up as we entered the room.

"Ah, Sherlock and Doctor Watson, come in. I have some news for you both."

"And that is?" Holmes asked, taking a seat before the desk and gesturing me to take the other. The chairs were old and well-polished, and obviously a match for the desk.

I think we were both expecting some piece of information or small clue. So the words that came out of Mycroft's mouth certainly startled me, but looking back, were unlikely to have surprised Holmes who knew his brother much better than I did.

"The needs of the Smythe children are being taken care of. The eldest boy now has a better-paying job than telegraph boy. The eldest girl is still in service with the vicar and his wife. They are good people and will not abuse her. The youngest two have been removed from the workhouse and have been placed in a good school." Mycroft pushed back his chair and rose from his desk to stand looking out the window towards the bulk of the Abbey.

"Mycroft!" Holmes voice was sharp with amusement.

"What?" Mycroft's tone was vaguely mulish.

"Pray tell who it is that is paying for all this?" Holmes asked.

"And why?" I added.

Mycroft refused to look at either of us, his attention firmly fixed on the looming walls of the Abbey. "Mrs. Smythe should not have died. In a tangential way, you could say she died on Diogenes business."

"Only if you stretch the concept as far as you can without it actually snapping," Holmes said dryly, but not without some gentle amusement.

Mycroft swung around and glared at him. "The school is run by a Diogenes Club member and takes deserving charity cases. As for the eldest boy, the telegraph office pays poorly, and there are too many temptations towards illicit gain." Mycroft glowered at us both, as if daring either of us to speak.

I could not help the chuckle that escaped me, as I realized here was one thing that the brothers had in common.

Neither of them cared to be caught doing something altruistic. Both brothers turned a baleful gaze on me, as they tracked my train of thought.

Mycroft snorted, and turned away. "Now I really must get to back to work."

"Yes, God forbid the government should have to get along without you for a few hours." Holmes' tone was one of amusement, as he rose from his seat.

Before Mycroft could respond, a lackey knocked and popped his head around the door. "Mr. Holmes, this came from Scotland Yard for your brother. Apparently he took it to Baker Street, but the landlady said he had come here. The lad who delivered it said it was a matter of some urgency."

Holmes took the message from him and tore it open. Seeing that Mycroft now had no intention of ushering us out until he had heard who the message was from, Holmes read it aloud. "Holmes, I am to be disciplined by Monro at 10 o'clock tomorrow morning for punching Watkins. Can you and Doctor Watson be at Scotland Yard as witnesses for me? Sincerely. G. Lestrade."

"What?" I yelled, thumping the back of the chair. I was furious. "Watkins thoroughly deserved that punch after he hit Dorothy. It is that animal that should be facing a disciplinary hearing, not Lestrade."

Holmes sighed. "I have told you before that the senior command does not like Lestrade. His desire for justice for everyone regardless of rank upsets those at the top who feel those in the gutter deserve nothing but contempt. They will use this as an excuse to rid themselves of Lestrade, and then sack Watkins."

Mycroft looked as grim as I felt. "You mean they will try to get rid of Lestrade."

Holmes turned to his brother, eyebrows raised in query.

"Lestrade has shown himself to be a good man and a good detective. Scotland Yard needs him more than they do some of the dunderheads at the top. Leave it with me. I will take care of it."

"You can persuade Monro not to continue with the hearing?" I asked.

"I can do a lot of things, Doctor Watson, just ask Sir Charles Warren."

"For the inspector's sake, I believe this hearing should go ahead. He deserves to see his alleged superiors grovel to him." Mycroft gave us a smile that was equal parts dark humour and outright evil, and sat back down at this desk. Taking this as a signal that the meeting was over, we left the office, shutting the door behind us.

"You know, Watson," Holmes said in a quiet conversational tone, once we were out of earshot of both Mycroft and his clerk, "I never liked it as a boy when Mycroft smiled like that."

"Oh?" I had to admit that the smile had unnerved me slightly.

"Yes. It usually meant that something unpleasant was about to occur to someone. Though it was always someone who deserved it, mind you. On one occasion the gardener hit one of the stable lads who stepped on his pansies by accident. Next day the gardener was found drunk and insensible lying in a pile of manure."

I could not see the connection, so I just gave Holmes an enquiring look.

A tight smile ghosted across Holmes' face. "The gardener never drank. Insisted his evening cocoa had been knobbled. Father did not believe him and fired him immediately. I went looking. One of my very first cases, you might say. I found only one thing."

"And that was?" I was curious now, despite myself.

"Mycroft's outdoor shoes almost spotlessly clean. Except for a tiny speck of manure that he had missed when cleaning them."

"Mycroft has always had a sense of justice and fair play, then?"

Holmes nodded. "He never says much. He never does much. But when he does, it feels as if all hell has broken loose from its moorings."

"Strange then that he should be so against female emancipation," I commented.

Holmes shrugged. "He has worked too long for the government. It has fossilized his thinking. If he truly sat and thought about it for a while he would see that it is the right and just thing to do."

"This case is pushing him, is it not?"

"It is pushing us all, to one degree or another. I know that you had met people like Sir Lucas and Dorothy before, but I had not, at least, not knowingly. This is very much as new to me as it is to Mycroft, and to Lestrade."

"Lestrade is coping marvelously well," I commented, "If his defense of Dorothy is anything to go by. And as for you." I paused, a smile twitching at the edge of my mouth, "Since when have your thought processes been anything but flexible?"

Holmes laughed. "I try, my dear Watson, I do try."

"You are often very trying," I agreed.

We hailed a cab and returned to Baker Street, where we settled back comfortably to read the morning newspapers.

Holmes selected a newspaper and then reached for the collection of yesterday's tobacco dottles that made up his morning pipe.

I picked up another paper and sat in my chair. Shaking out the pages, I looked across at Holmes. "What do you plan to do today? Will you take that button to Mrs. Bradstreet?"

"I was considering such a visit, but I do not believe it would be prudent to do so."

"Why not?" I was curious. It was not like Holmes to not immediately follow up on such a major find.

"Until we have got Lestrade out from under the cloud of this spurious hearing, I do not wish to do anything that may jeopardize his position. Besides, I strongly suspect that there will be police officers around the house to prevent us visiting. I rather like the idea of them waiting all day in vain." Holmes' smile was positively vicious.

"So, a quiet day in then?" I asked.

"Just so," Holmes replied.

We read in silence for a while. I lowered my paper and looked across at Holmes. He was deep into the current copy of the Police Gazette.

"Holmes."

"What is it, Watson?"

"I do not understand Watkins' role in all this. Why did he hit Dorothy? Why call her such dreadful names?"

"It really is obvious, Watson," Holmes said in a long-suffering tone, from behind the Gazette.

"Not to me it is not," I replied tartly.

Holmes lowered his paper and looked at me. "Wiggins saw Watkins in Cleveland Street during the fire. Watkins was the first officer to arrive upon the scene of Daisy's killing."

"Yes."

"Ask yourself this: why was he in both places? It is obvious."

"It is not obvious to me!"

"The man is the lookout man for our killer."

"What? How on earth did you arrive at such a conclusion?"

Holmes gave me a look of irritation. "Mostly it was his behaviour towards Dorothy. The foul accusations and the assault. Dorothy does not dress like a street whore, but like the genteel lady that she is. Watkins must have known that she had lived at the Cleveland Street house and thought, as we did originally, that the inhabitants were all whores."

"I follow that," I said.

"Good! Now. Watkins is based out of A Division. An area that does not cover Cleveland Street. He had no reason to be there."

"Maybe he lives there?"

Holmes shook his head. "No. I had a word with the sergeant last night. Watkins lives close to the station with his mother. Therefore he had no legitimate reason to be in Cleveland Street on the night of the fire. As I said last night, what we need to discover is what links Watkins with Nathaniel Croft."

"Perhaps Mrs. Bradstreet will be able to tell us when we eventually get to visit her."

"A good thought, Watson. Perhaps she will." With that, Holmes picked up his paper again and refused to speak another word.

Chapter Thirteen

I awoke the next morning to a sound rarely heard in our rooms at that hour, indeed, at any hour. Holmes was laughing. Deep belly laughs interspersed with the occasional snigger.

Curious, I did not wait to dress, but wrapped my dressing gown around myself, and ventured out into the main room.

Holmes was seated at the table with an array of periodicals spread around him. He looked up at my entrance and grinned widely.

"Good morning, my dear Watson. I see my brother has excelled himself." He waved a copy of The Times at me.

I took the paper from him. A sedate article, halfway down the second column, decried Scotland Yard's abysmal treatment of the "gallant and chivalrous" Inspector Lestrade, whose behaviour in defense of a lady was a shining example for all young policemen to aspire to.

I looked at Holmes. "This is your brother's method?"

Holmes' grin widened. "Embarrassment can be an extremely effective weapon, Watson. And one Mycroft knows well how to wield." The grin turned vicious, "And while The Times is being genteel and gentlemanly about it all, other periodicals are less so."

He truffled around amongst the papers, waving the ones he found at me. "The Illustrated London News calls Monro and Anderson "ungrateful troglodytes who could not detect the skin on a rice pudding"."

Holmes paused. "I admit that I am impressed. I had not realized there was anyone at the News that could even spell troglodyte, let alone know what the word means."

"The phrasing most likely came verbatim from Mycroft," I suggested.

Holmes thought about it for a moment. "You may very well be right, my friend, that does sound rather like him."

He dug out more newspapers. "The Daily Telegraph is of the opinion that Lestrade's abilities and eye for justice are an embarrassment to his superiors. They are well on the mark with that one. They have also mentioned that Lestrade is due to be disciplined today."

"Well, that should guarantee a nice turnout at Scotland Yard," I said drily.

Holmes smiled. "Oh yes. I suspect Lestrade will get a hero's welcome when he arrives."

"He will find that even more embarrassing than this farce of a hearing," I observed.

"All too true, Watson. Here." Holmes held out another periodical. The smile on his face was wicked. "I am afraid this will not do much to ease his embarrassment, either."

I took a copy of Punch magazine from him, I stared for a few moments then began to laugh helplessly. Punch's illustrators had created a wickedly clever cartoon. Lestrade was depicted as a knight in shining armour protecting a damsel in distress from a dragon clad in a police constable's uniform. A wicked caricature indeed.

I looked at the mess of papers spread over the table. "Is there any breakfast under there?"

Holmes began to remove the papers, "Not yet. I asked Mrs. Hudson to wait until you had risen before bringing it."

"And I will serve it, if someone will get that mess off of the table," the lady in question said tartly from the doorway, where she stood carrying a heavy breakfast tray. The twinkle in her eyes belied the sharpness of her tone.

I hurried to take the tray from her, as Holmes continued to clear the table of the detritus of journalistic endeavour.

As I savoured my breakfast, I thought about the day ahead. I was hoping that Mycroft's methods would not backfire on poor Lestrade.

"I would not worry, if I were you, Watson. Lestrade will come out of this, if not smelling of roses, then redolent of something equally as sweet."

"Reading my mind again?"

Holmes shrugged. "I do like a little light reading in the morning."

It was obvious that the output of the morning's newspapers had put him in one of his rare mischievous moods.

I glared at him around the slice of toast I had in my mouth.

He smiled at my expression. "Your worried expression and frequent glances to where I had placed the papers told me what you were thinking."

Holmes grew serious. "Mycroft well knows the way the minds of these Home Office appointed men work. They will be seriously discommoded by the newspaper reports this morning. Especially as it signals that neither Monro nor Anderson is doing his job properly. Both men are good men. But Anderson is not inclined to challenge the status quo, and Monro is more concerned about the lower ranks than those of the middle and upper. Which is a fine position to take, until one of those ranks needs his support. Both men would conceivably partake in human sacrifice if it meant everything ran smoothly and without controversy."

"If they remove Lestrade from his position, then human sacrifice is precisely what they will have done," I replied.

"Lestrade will not lose his position." Holmes voice was full of resolve.

"How can you know that?" I challenged.

"Mycroft will have made sure that Her Majesty gets this morning's papers and learns an edited version of Lestrade's exploits. Her Majesty does have a soft spot for gallant gentlemen. I am sure that by the time the hearing begins, Monro will have learned of Her Majesty's opinion on events. That will colour his behaviour and responses accordingly. It will work much better than Mycroft obviously pulling strings."

Holmes smiled, then snatched the last piece of toast before I could. I glared at him. He gave me an increasing smug smile from behind the slice of toast and marmalade. I took the last boiled egg in response.

We caught a cab to Scotland Yard, though we had to abandon it at the top of Whitehall Place, due to the sizeable crowd that had gathered outside the Yard's building itself.

Uniformed police officers were lining the street directly outside, under the watchful eye of Sergeant Halliday, who was not allowing them to respond to the jeers about uniformed brutes and animals.

As we carefully pushed our way up the street, I heard him say sharply to one young constable, "None of us likes Watkins. He gives us all a bad name. Men like him have no business wearing the uniform. Now stop your whining."

"Well put, Sergeant," Holmes said breezily. "Has Inspector Lestrade arrived yet?"

Sergeant Halliday swung around to us, a surprised expression on his face, which quickly cleared when he saw who it was.

"No, Mr. Holmes. But expect we'll know he's coming before we see him." He gestured at the crowd.

Holmes' lips twitched into a brief smile. "No doubt. I do not think the good Inspector will be expecting this sort of turn out in his support."

Sergeant Halliday gave Holmes a sharp look. "Did you arrange this, sir?" he asked.

"Do I look like the sort of man who could raise a crowd in such a fashion?"

"No sir, but if Doctor Watson's stories are true, and I know that they are, then you are the sort of man to know men who could do this."

"Sergeant Halliday has you there, Holmes," I observed.

I took the opportunity to ask Halliday about Archie.

Halliday beamed at me. "He's settling in well, doctor. Thank you for asking. The wife's taken to him well. She used to be a governess before we married. When she found out he wants to be a policeman, she offered to teach him to read, and write, and do sums. Made me dig out her old schoolbooks from the attic, and they're making a start at it this morning."

Holmes looked concerned, no doubt about Archie being left unprotected with a woman.

Halliday interpreted the look. "Don't worry about the lad, sir. He'll be safe. Even if Watkins knew where I lived, Bobby would see him off."

"Bobby?" I asked.

Halliday grinned. "He's the latest in a long line of large, mongrel, dogs. Part mastiff, part something bloody big and hairy. The wife doesn't like being left alone when I'm on night duty. Dog's well trained. Nothing gets through the door when I'm not at home. Bobby took to Archie as well. Spent last night sleeping at the end of his bed."

"Seems like Archie is well-served all round," I said quietly.

"He's a good lad. Full of questions. Lively as a box of ferrets. It's a pleasure to have him."

We moved away to allow Halliday to get on with his job. Holmes looked well-pleased. I eyed him carefully. "Pleased about Archie?" I asked.

Holmes smiled warmly, "Oh yes! Archie is a bright lad. He deserves every chance he can get. Mostly, though, I am extremely pleased at the turnout here. I do suspect that this has surpassed even Mycroft's expectations."

I gazed across the street at the gathered crowd. The feeling was not hostile, despite the jibes at the constables. There was an air of anticipation, and I realized that everyone was waiting for Lestrade to arrive. I glanced at my fob watch.

It was twenty minutes from the hour. Lestrade should be along shortly.

The cheering started at one end of Whitehall Place. Listening carefully I could hear voices calling out things like: "There he is!" and "Our hero!" Then someone began to chant, and the rest of the crowd picked it up: "Lestrade! Lestrade! Lestrade!"

Inspector Lestrade came into view, coming along Whitehall Place from the end where we had entered. He was pink-cheeked with an air of complete bewilderment. A young lass, no more than sixteen, popped out from the crowd and handed him a rose, kissing his cheek lightly before disappearing into the mass. Lestrade blushed a deep red.

I heard Halliday snort with amusement. I was hard-pressed not to laugh out loud myself. Holmes was as inscrutable as ever.

As if the lass had been a signal, flowers started to fly from the crowd. Simple flowers such as those that can be bought from any flower seller along the Strand or Covent Garden: daisies, violets, pansies, and the occasional rose.

"I hope they have removed the thorns," I murmured. "Otherwise they could do Lestrade a nasty injury."

Holmes did not respond.

Lestrade came up to us, his blushes not even beginning to fade. He glared at Holmes. "Did you do this?" He waved at the crowd, who cheered and waved back with increased enthusiasm.

"Not me, my friend, my brother seems to want you to remain at Scotland Yard."

Lestrade looked startled. "Mycroft Holmes? But why? He barely knows me."

"Mycroft Holmes is very like his brother," I said. "He sees much that others do not, and is an excellent judge of people's characters."

"Watson's description of my brother is, essentially, correct."

Lestrade sighed. "Let us take this inside gentleman, and get this damned farce over with."

Together the three of us mounted the steps and walked into the great bastion of justice that is Scotland Yard.

Inside hurrying constables and sergeants seemed not to know how to respond to Lestrade. There were a few supportive smiles, but most seemed to be sitting on the fence. When I commented on it, with some surprise, Lestrade's response was a derisive snort.

"Most members of Her Majesty's glorious London Metropolitan Police are not capable of independent thought, Doctor. They are waiting to see what Monro wants them to think."

"You do not appear to care for your fellow officers much," I observed. I remembered meeting him with Inspector Tobias Gregson in the first case of Sherlock Holmes' that I recorded as "A Study in Scarlet." There had been no love lost between the two men, and, I admit, at the time, I had disliked both men. Lestrade, however, had grown upon me as I had got to know him better. I still did not care much for Gregson, who I was sure was around here somewhere ready to gloat if things turned out badly for the little inspector.

"Have you considered becoming a consulting detective, like Holmes?" I asked, genuinely curious.

Lestrade paused and looked at me. He appeared to be searching for words. "Holmes does much good in this city," he said at last, "He gets justice for people where he can. But he cannot bring a man to lawful trial. Justice has to be done, Doctor Watson, but it also has to be seen to be done. Holmes has to perforce work too much in the shadows for me to be comfortable doing the same." He looked down the corridor where we were walking towards a large mahogany door. Lestrade's distaste for the situation showed on his face. "Now, as I said outside, let us get this farce over with."

He strode confidentially towards the door, which had a large, uniformed sergeant standing in front of it. Holmes and I followed silently behind. Seeing us coming, the sergeant opened the door, spoke to someone inside, and then stood aside to allow us to enter.

The room was large and well-furnished, with a highly polished oak desk dominating the room. A man aged around fifty, with receding hair and chin, solid and blocky, sat at the desk. Standing behind him was a man of similar age with a somewhat bulbous nose and rather small eyes. Commissioner James Monro, and Assistant Commissioner (Head of Detectives) Robert Anderson.

Individually, they did not look like much, but as a duo they were a powerful combination. Monro had been the head of the Special Irish Branch with Anderson his deputy. During the Queen's jubilee in 1887, they had foiled a Fenian attempt to blow up Westminster Abbey. Holmes might consider them fools on some level, but the reality was both men were far from foolish. Both men were highly intelligent, each with a strong moral compass, even though Anderson was given to occasional bursts of what appeared to be a startling lack of judgment.

At the beginning of the Ripper outrage, Anderson had gone away on holiday and had to be dragged back from France after a month! Paired with Sir Charles Warren the duo had made a pig's breakfast of the investigation. When Warren had been replaced with Monro, the heroes of Westminster had not been able to solve the case due to a number of factors including incorrect gathering of evidence, destruction of evidence, and, in part, downright incompetence on the behalf of officers in the field. I knew it frustrated Holmes that he had been kept from the case, as had Lestrade, because of his working relationship with Holmes. Freddie Abberline was a good detective, but it had been a case of far too little, far too late. By the time the senior officers at Scotland Yard took the crimes seriously, the investigation had been botched beyond repair.

Monro rose from his seat and reached across the desk to shake our hands. Anderson stepped forward to do the same. I wondered if this boded good or ill for Lestrade.

Monro waved to three chairs that the sergeant from outside and two constables had brought in behind us. "Take a seat, gentlemen."

Holmes and I seated ourselves one on each side of Lestrade. He flashed us a quick look, and I gave him a reassuring smile. Lestrade smiled back briefly before turning his attention to the man across the desk.

"This is a sorry situation, Giles," said Monro. "We have had a second, somewhat more serious complaint filed."

"Against me?" Lestrade asked sharply.

"No." It was Anderson who spoke. "Against Constable Watkins."

"It seems," said Monro, "That the lady Watkins assaulted has some connection to Sir Lucas Catterick."

Lestrade nodded. "You could say that she is the ward of one of his cousins."

Monro looked down at a letter on his desk. "It appears that she is one Dorothy Watts, companion to his elderly grandmother…"

"That good lady, Commissioner," said Holmes, "Lady Caroline Harkness, is one lady you really do not want to cross. The lady may be old, but she still has all her wits about her, and no doubt still has many influential connections."

Monro's expression was sour. "So I have been told, Mr. Holmes. I have also been informed by Sir Lucas that Miss Watts does good works amongst the unfortunates of the streets." He looked down at the papers on his desk.

"So why are you sniping at Lestrade, one of the finest officers you have, instead of sacking that miserable excuse for a policeman, Watkins?" My tone held acid. Both Holmes and Lestrade gazed at me. Holmes with an eyebrow raised; Lestrade with something that resembled shock.

Monro looked across at me. "A valid question, Doctor Watson. We walk a fine line here. There is never enough money to police this city properly. Politicians begrudge us every penny for wages for our men, and for expenses to investigate crimes. Every shilling has to be damn near squeezed out of the Home Office."

"The Home Office wanted an excuse to stop the investigation into what they saw less as murder and more as pest control," Anderson added, his tone blunt. "Inspector Lestrade is viewed as a major liability due to his interesting notions on fairness and justice for all." The hint of the smile around Anderson's mouth suggested that he shared at least some of Lestrade's notions.

"You were told close down the investigation and take the golden opportunity to rid yourselves of Lestrade?" Holmes own tone held disgust.

"Essentially, yes," agreed Monro. "Though I refuse to get rid of as good an officer as Lestrade. I would have found something else to occupy his time." He paused for a moment, "And not taken any notice if he had decided to assist you in your own ongoing efforts to solve the case, Mr. Holmes."

My friend broke into a tight smile. "And there is the reason why you were chosen to replace Sir Charles Warren, Commissioner."

Monro waved the comment off. "This morning I received a communication from the Home Office."

Anderson snorted. "An extremely panicked communication. Some people fairly high in the ranks came to the sudden, somewhat abrupt, realization that their priorities and those of other, more important people, shall we say, do not coincide."

Holmes eyed Anderson and Monro blandly. "Her Majesty saw this morning's little output from the newspapers."

Monro looked Holmes square in the eyes. "I understand that someone she trusts implicitly delivered the papers to her personally."

I held back a smile at the thought of Mycroft Holmes acting as a newspaper boy.

"So what happens now?" Lestrade asked.

Monro looked at him. "You continue your investigation into these murders. I fully endorse the involvement of Mr. Holmes and Doctor Watson in the investigation. Both men have proven valuable to Scotland Yard before. I understand that there may have been developments?"

Lestrade looked at Holmes, signaling for him to take up the thread.

"There have," Holmes confirmed. "Miss Watts gave us an excellent description of the man that she and the boy saw kill the last victim. And a clue that poor unfortunate provided has led to the identification of the killer."

Monro and Anderson both started and stared at Holmes in shock.

"Any chance of an arrest?" Anderson asked eagerly.

Holmes smiled coldly. "I perceive there to be every chance."

"Who?" Monro asked.

"The killer looks to be a man named Nathaniel Croft. His sister can identify an item found in the hand of Daisy Macklin. If she confirms what I suspect, then we will need only to find where he is, to get him. That should not prove to be too onerous a task."

"Where does the sister fit into this, Mr. Holmes?" Anderson asked, brows drawn down in confusion.

"Her husband was the third victim," Holmes said quietly.

"God Lord!" Anderson was aghast. "The lady was married to…" He paused, obviously looking for suitable words.

Holmes gave him a look filled with contempt. "No. Her husband worked for someone in a fashion that required him to pose as something he was not." He looked away from Anderson to Monro, his eyes cold and hard. "I believe that you take my meaning, Commissioner."

Monro looked like he had found half a worm in his apple. "I had wondered why he was involved. My predecessor learned the futility of going up against your brother the hard way, Mr. Holmes. I am neither stupid nor suicidal. All the power of the London Metropolitan Police will be at your disposal when you need it. All I ask is that you let Lestrade have the credit."

"I do not seek glory, unlike some of your officers. Lestrade is more than welcome to any kudos that may accrue from our endeavor."

Monro nodded.

"And Watkins?" I asked.

"By the end of today Andrew Watkins will no longer be a member of Her Majesty's London Metropolitan Police," Monro replied. "We need more like Lestrade and considerably fewer like Watkins."

Holmes rose to his feet, and Lestrade and I followed him. Wishing Monro and Anderson a brisk good day, we strode from the office.

Gregson was lurking in the stairwell as we headed downstairs. "How did it go, Lestrade?" I could see he was gleefully anticipating his rival's downfall. My dislike for the man crept up a notch.

Holmes clapped Gregson on the shoulder, all good humour and false bon homie. "You will be pleased to know, Gregson, that the Commissioner has decided to sack that violent incompetent Watkins, has confirmed Lestrade's role in the investigation, and committed the entirety of Her Majesty's London Metropolitan Police to the investigation. A good morning's work, eh?"

Gregson mumbled something vaguely congratulatory and scuttled away. Lestrade smirked after his retreating back.

He turned to Holmes. "Back to visit Mrs. Bradstreet, then?"

"Of course, where else would we be going?"

Whitehall Place was a different experience compared to our earlier arrival. Most of the crowd had dispersed. Lestrade looked around. Sergeant Halliday came up to him, chuckling. "One of the superintendents came out and announced you had been cleared and that Watkins had been sacked. Everyone headed for the nearest pubs to celebrate."

"London's reaction to any news, good or bad," Holmes observed, "...is to have a drink."

"The local publicans will be blessing Lestrade's name by close of business," I said drily. "Perhaps we should join them?"

"Begging your pardon. Doctor, but I think you might have another appointment," said Halliday. He held out a heavy cream coloured envelope to Holmes. "A messenger in green and gold livery delivered this while you were with the Commissioner. Said you were to be handed it as soon as you came out."

Holmes opened the envelope. A piece of good quality card, that matched the envelope, slid out. Written on it in a firm hand were the words: Come to the Diogenes Club upon receipt. M.

"Looks like your brother wishes to know what happened," said Lestrade.

Holmes smiled, a little grimly, I thought. "My brother already knows what occurred in there. He arranged it after all. Mark my words, there will be another reason for the summons. Though he should really be at Whitehall at this time of the day. Mycroft is a law unto himself. The hours he keeps are for his convenience, not that of other people."

"Well, we can still have a drink, but at Mycroft's expense, and the Diogenes Club is sure to have a better cellar than any of the local pubs will," I said.

"Good old Watson," Holmes' tone held a faint trace of amusement. "Straight to the point as always."

Chapter Fourteen

We walked up Whitehall Place and hailed a cab near Trafalgar Square. We sat in silence for a few moments: Holmes lost in his own thoughts and Lestrade no doubt contemplating his near brush with unemployment. I was ruminating over the events in Monro's office, when I realized that I had learned something this morning. I looked across at Lestrade sitting opposite me.

"I did not know that your name is Giles."

"There is a lot about Lestrade you do not know, Watson."

"Oh? I suppose that you knew his first name?"

Holmes shrugged. "It was not hard to find out. I do like to know with whom I am working."

Lestrade's eyebrows shot skywards. "You investigated me?"

"Naturally. Too many of your colleagues are useless dunderheads. I did not want to saddle myself with someone whose only interest was arresting someone, regardless of whether they were actually guilty of the crime in question or not. You, my dear Lestrade, have the makings of an excellent detective."

"Scotland Yard already pays him to be a detective," I pointed out.

"They also employ people to empty the slop buckets."

"Junior constables usually do that," Lestrade observed mildly, "Not to mention making the tea."

Holmes ignored his interjection. "The point is, they may employ you to be a detective, but unless you have the intelligence and the skills, you will never be better than the bumblers who worked the torso killings. How they could not discover the killer who placed a dismembered corpse in the very foundations of the new Scotland Yard building on the Embankment is beyond anyone of even the smallest amount of intelligence."

"Anderson was in charge of that, was he not?" I asked.

Holmes response was icy. "I rest my case."

Lestrade laughed nastily. I ignored it. The man could be excused for thinking less than charitably about one of the men who had been willing to end his career.

The cab stopped outside the Diogenes Club. Holmes paid the fare, and we entered the club rooms. A young man in the club's livery met us as the door. Holmes scrutinized his face carefully, then smiled to himself, gesturing for the lad to escort us to the Stranger's Room, where Mycroft was waiting for us.

Mycroft was pouring champagne into four glasses as we entered. Holmes raised his eyebrows. "It is a trifle little early for that, surely, Mycroft?"

"Nonsense, Sherlock. It is never too early to celebrate a well-executed plan."

"Mycroft handed a glass to Lestrade, and then one to me. He picked up his own, leaving the fourth one for his brother.

"A toast," Mycroft said with a slight smile, "...to Inspector Lestrade's continued employment with the London Metropolitan Police."

Lestrade's ears went pink, and both Holmes and I mumbled some sort of response. I sipped the wine for politeness sake. I am not enthused by alcohol except a good brandy or port or the occasional beer. Holmes is a connoisseur of wine, but I had not seen him drink champagne before.

Mycroft set his glass down on the table. "Now that that has been taken care of, what is the next step?"

Holmes set his glass beside his brother's. "The next step is to visit Mrs. Bradstreet again. We have found something that if she recognizes it then we know who our killer is and we merely have to net him."

Mycroft raised his eyebrows. "What did you find?"

Holmes put his hand into his pocket and brought out the scrap of lace with the button attached. Mycroft gazed at it, brows drawn down in concentration.

"A button?" he finally asked.

Holmes nodded, returning the object to his pocket. "When we last spoke with Mrs. Bradstreet she gave us a detailed description of a dress that had gone missing from the trunk where it was stored. The button I just showed you came from a dress that matches the description of the missing garment."

"A garment that was being worn by a man masquerading as a woman," Lestrade added, no doubt feeling it was his duty as a police officer to at least say something.

Mycroft was silent for a while, putting the pieces together. He nodded to himself, as if confirming something. "Jeremiah's killer was his brother-in-law, Nathaniel."

"Not just Jeremiah's killer. But also the killer of the poor unfortunates. Tell, me Mycroft, was Jeremiah working the night he was murdered?" Holmes asked.

"Yes. He had been to another of Mrs. Cunningham's meetings."

"Good Lord!" I could not help the exclamation. The Holmes brothers turned to me with identical looks of enquiry. "Bradstreet must have been returning home still in his disguise, and seen the killer."

"And, more importantly," Lestrade added, following my train of thought, "recognized him. So Bradstreet had to die."

Both Holmeses smiled at us, like benevolent school masters upon particularly bright pupils.

"What will you do if Nathaniel is at home?" Mycroft asked. "Confronting him at the house might well endanger his sister."

"I do not think he will be present," Holmes said. "When we last spoke with Mrs. Bradstreet she said Nathaniel had returned to work at his tailor's shop on Marylebone High Street. Once we have confirmation, then we shall confront him there."

"With a large number of uniformed officers," Lestrade added. "We do not want him even considering trying to get away."

"Excellent." Mycroft beamed at us. "It looks as if it is all coming together at last."

Taking it for the dismissal it clearly was, Lestrade and I put down our glasses and joined Holmes at the door. As we were leaving, Holmes turned back and looked at Mycroft.

"I see the Diogenes Club has a new usher, Mycroft."

Mycroft looked back, as if daring his brother to continue.

"I did wonder where you had placed the eldest Smythe boy. I am sure he will be much happier working here than at the telegraph office." Bestowing a beaming smile upon Mycroft, Holmes walked away, leaving Lestrade and I to follow.

"The eldest Smythe boy?" Lestrade asked as we left the club.

"You told us about Evelyn Smythe's family when she was murdered," I reminded Lestrade.

Lestrade nodded. "Ah! Yes! The eldest girl was working for a vicar, and the eldest boy in the telegraph office." His face clouded. "The two youngest were sent to the workhouse."

Holmes turned to Lestrade, nodding his head in my direction. "Watson here waxed lyrical about the injustice of it all in front of Mycroft, who, though he would steadfastly deny it, actually does have a heart."

"Can you stop being clever for one minute and just tell me what happened?" Lestrade's tone was slightly cross. The man had had a very trying morning.

"Mycroft intervened," Holmes replied. "The eldest girl remains in service at the vicarage. The vicar and his wife have been investigated and are sound, compassionate, people who will not abuse her. Telegraph office wages are nothing but a pittance, so Mycroft hired the lad to work at the Diogenes Club. Before you say anything, it is obvious just looking at the lad that he is Evelyn Smythe's son. The evidence is in the shape of the nose and the sweep of the jawline. Mycroft also prevailed upon another Diogenes member who runs a charity school to take the two youngest. They no longer reside in the workhouse and will get a useful education."

Lestrade cocked his head and stared thoughtfully at my friend.

"What is it, Lestrade?" Holmes asked, somewhat testily.

"I wonder who it was that investigated the vicar and his wife?"

The slight flush that stained Holmes' cheeks gave us the response to that question.

"It seems that Mycroft is not the only one with a heart," I observed quietly.

"Holmes ignored me in favour of hailing a cab and giving the driver the address in Putney.

It was slightly after noon when we arrived at the Bradstreet house, and the cool of the morning was giving way to what promised to be a fine, warm, afternoon. Mary answered our knock, settled us in the parlour, and went to fetch her mistress.

Viola Bradstreet soon joined us, taking each of our hands in turn as we rose from our chairs to greet her. She arranged herself comfortably on the small settee and looked at us enquiringly as we retook out seats.

"There has been a development," Holmes said quietly. "One that may tell us who murdered your husband, but, equally, it may cause you great distress."

"You have me both intrigued and worried, Mr. Holmes," Viola replied.

Holmes put his hand in his pocket out and brought out the scrap of lace with the attached button. He held it out in the palm of his hand towards Mrs. Bradstreet. "Do you recognize this?" His voice was gentle.

Viola stared at the button with what could almost be described as incomprehension. She raised her eyes to look at Holmes. Her expression was wide and vulnerable. "Mary," she said, her voice shaking slightly, "Please fetch my sewing box."

The girl bobbed a small curtsey. "Yes, ma'am."

Mary disappeared from the room to return with a large cloth covered box that was embroidered all over with brightly coloured flowers. She placed the box in Viola Bradstreet's lap.

Mrs. Bradstreet opened it and sorted through the contents for a moment. Then she withdrew something from the box and held it out in the palm of her hand, placing her hand next to that of Holmes. It was a button. Identical to the one Holmes had recovered from Daisy's hand.

"Where did you find the button, Mr. Holmes?"

Holmes sighed. "In the hand of a murder victim. It was torn from off her killer's gown."

Mary stifled a gasp. "A woman killed the master?"

Holmes shook his head. His eyes were still on Mrs. Bradstreet.

She bowed her head for a long while. When she raised it, she gazed at us with steely eyes, though they were filmed with tears. Her lips trembled slightly, but her voice was firm when she spoke.

"It was Nathaniel."

The sentence was a statement, not a question.

"We believe so, ma'am."

"Why?"

"That is the one thing we are not sure about," Lestrade said. "We need to speak to him."

Mrs. Bradstreet turned to look at him. "Nathaniel should be at his shop on Marylebone High Street, or in his lodgings above it." She then gave us the address.

Lestrade got to his feet and hurried from the room. I heard the front door open and shut and his footsteps as he raced down the path.

"Nathaniel has not come to live here?" Holmes asked.

She shook her head. "No. This house was mine and Jeremiah's home. Michael lived in rooms in Westminster, and Nathaniel has his lodgings in Marylebone. Nathaniel was staying with me in the aftermath of Michael's death and then Jeremiah's murder."

Her expression changed to one of anger. "He murdered my husband and he stayed with me, playing at the grieving brother. Why?"

Holmes cleared his throat. "He could do nothing else. Any other behaviour would have cast him in a less the auspicious light. If it is any consolation, I do not believe he deliberately targeted your husband. I believe Jeremiah Bradstreet was in the wrong place at the wrong time and saw something he should not have."

Given her grief, Viola Bradstreet was surprisingly perspicacious, making me understand how her husband and her other brother had not been able to keep their occupation secret.

"Nathaniel is the Molly-Boy Killer."

Holmes nodded. "I believe so, ma'am."

"In God's name…why?"

"That I cannot tell you," Holmes held up a hand in gentled admonition. "But only because I do not know for certain, but once we have him we shall find out more."

"Please let me know. I need to know why my brother has done what he did." Her puzzlement eased into a frown. "At least I know what happened to the dress."

"Indeed ma'am," Holmes said. "Given that it had more material than the current fashion allows for, it was ideal for Nathaniel to tailor it to fit himself."

Lestrade came back in; he had a uniformed constable with him. "I have sent the cabbie to Scotland Yard to get us some more bodies. I do not want it just to be the three of us. I would feel more comfortable, for once, surrounded by uniforms."

He introduced the constable with him. "This is Constable Cole, Mrs. Bradstreet. He is the officer who patrols around here. I intercepted him and brought him here. He will stay with you in case Nathaniel gets away and tries to come to you. I want you to be safe."

Constable Cole was about the same height as Nathaniel Croft, but broader across the shoulders, and looked like he could handle himself if the killer came to call.

"Thank you, Inspector. I appreciate your concern."

Lestrade looked at Holmes and myself. "I have another cab waiting outside, shall we go?"

"Have you let Constable Cole's superiors know where he is?" I asked.

"I thought I would get the cabbie to call into the Putney station on the way to Marylebone."

"Excellent. It seems you have thought of everything, Lestrade. Let us be going then," said Holmes.

We took brief farewells of Mrs. Bradstreet, Mary, and Constable Cole, then went out to the street where the cab was waiting patiently for us.

We turned back as Viola Bradstreet called us from the doorstep.

"Mr. Holmes, it was Nathaniel who cleared out Michael's lodgings in Westminster. His behaviour became a little strange after that."

"Exactly how strange was his behaviour?" asked Holmes.

"Nathaniel and Michael were both very open, light-hearted, people. Always prepared to have a laugh with you. Gently teasing family and friends. They used to impersonate each other as boys. But after Michael died, Nathaniel became closed off and brooding. I thought it was because they were twins. Then I wondered if Nathaniel had taken to drink. Either way, I did not have the heart to chide him for his behaviour. Even though it was hard for me to deal with. Then after Jeremiah was killed, Nathaniel would barely look me in the eye. After your first visit he fled back to his lodgings leaving Mary, Cook, and I to cope alone."

"Thank you, Mrs. Bradstreet." Holmes turned away.

"Mr. Holmes!"

He turned back, brows raised in query.

"Nathaniel is going to hang, isn't he?"

"It depends on the jury, ma'am." It was Lestrade who replied. "He may very well be found to be insane and spend the rest of his life in Broadmoor."

Viola's eyes ghosted with tears. "God help me, but I think I would rather he was hanged."

The three of us bowed our heads, and Lestrade and I headed again for the cab. Holmes gently patted Mrs. Bradstreet's hands before joining us in the cab. As we drove away I looked back and saw Mary and another woman, who I assumed was the cook, leading Viola Bradstreet back into the house. Constable Cole stood firmly on the front step.

Chapter Fifteen

We stopped briefly at the Putney police station, where Lestrade informed the duty sergeant of the whereabouts of his constable, before we set off at a brisk trot back towards Marylebone.

Holmes sank into his brooding trance, whilst Lestrade and I kept up a light chatter, much to Holmes' annoyance. We were both too keyed up at the prospect of cornering our killer to take much notice of Holmes' introspection.

"I do find it hard to believe that Mycroft Holmes went out of his way to help the Smythe orphans," said Lestrade. "He just does not seem the type."

Holmes snorted, obviously having given up on the possibility of thinking in silence. "I hardly think you are one to talk, Lestrade."

"What do you mean?" I asked.

"Lestrade gives up his valuable time away from policing to help out at the Metropolitan and City Police Orphanage in Twickenham. Plays cricket and football with the boys, I understand."

Lestrade went faintly pink.

"I did say I had investigated you," Holmes reminded him.

"I did not realize that you had been that thorough."

"When I say I have investigated someone, you can be sure that I know almost everything there is to know about the person."

"Almost everything?" I asked.

"Some trifle is always missed, Watson. It really is not possible to know absolutely everything about a person."

"Even me?" I challenged.

Holmes smiled slightly. "In some ways, my friend, you are one of the biggest mysteries of all."

"And why, pray tell, is that?"

"Most people conform to the roles that society has assigned them, whether or not it is of conscious volition. There is a certain perception as to the usual and acceptable behaviours for, say, doctors in private practice. You, my dear Watson, do not totally conform to these unwritten rules. It makes anticipating your reactions to stimuli interesting, to say the very least."

We continued our ride in a slightly lighter mood. Lestrade assured us that the constables from Scotland Yard would wait for our arrival before attempting to arrest Nathaniel Croft.

"They would be wise to be cautious," Holmes said. "We do know that he carries a knife."

"Would a knife be effective against several large constables carrying truncheons?" Lestrade asked, with a hint of sarcasm.

"Pray that we do not have cause to find out," Holmes replied.

Nathaniel Croft's working premises were in a tidy little shop close to Devonshire Street. Six burly young constables and an equally young, though slightly less burly, sergeant were waiting for us. A police wagon was waiting beside the kerb.

The horses standing with the complete patience and calmness of police horses everywhere.

A small alley ran down the side of the block that housed Nathaniel's premises. Holmes' sharp eyes caught a movement.

"You! There! Come out at once!"

A figure slid out of shadows of the alley. It was a man with his head down, hunched into a slightly overlarge coat. It took me a moment to realize that the man was Watkins, hopefully by now, former Constable of the London Metropolitan Police.

Lestrade strode across the road towards him. "Watkins," he barked. "What are you doing here?"

"Nothing," came the sullen response.

Lestrade snorted his contempt. "Well go and do 'nothing' elsewhere. We have business here." He turned his back on Watkins to call across to the sergeant.

Watkins fumbled with an inside pocket of his coat, and his right hand emerged holding a police issue truncheon. He raised it high, aiming straight for Lestrade's head. Lestrade's bowler hat offered no protection against that vicious club.

"Lestrade!" I roared. "Look out!"

Lestrade half turned, and dodged nimbly to his left, as Watkins completed his swing. The head of the truncheon connected with Lestrade's right shoulder. He fell backwards and sideways, and hissed with pain as he jarred his shoulder against the wall of the alley.

Watkins raised his truncheon again

All seven police officers had begun to run across the road to Lestrade's aid. But Holmes was quicker than all of them. He leaped behind Watkins, grasping the man's left wrist in his hands, and forcing the arm up behind Watkins' back.

Watkins attempted to shake him off, but Holmes was both strong and tenacious. He twisted viciously on Watkins' arm, causing the man to shriek with pain. "Drop your weapon, or, by God, I will break your arm. Drop it! Now!" Holmes' voice held a note of command that I had rarely heard from him before.

Whining like a kicked cur, Watkins dropped the truncheon onto the ground. Holmes released his arm and stood back. Immediately Watkins was swarmed under by the police officers, who hauled him to his feet and handcuffed him, ignoring his whimpers of pain.

Holmes helped Lestrade to his feet. I hurried to join them. Lestrade was clutching his shoulder and muttering expletives under his breath.

I pushed Holmes out of the way. Lestrade tried to shy away from me. "Stop that! Let me look. You may need hospital."

Lestrade growled something I chose to ignore, as, with Holmes' assistance I got Lestrade out of his coat. Gentle prodding and flexing of the shoulder by me prompted growls and hisses of pain from Lestrade. I was relieved to find that the shoulder was not broken. "Deep bruising only, Inspector. You will be as right as rain in a week to ten days." I said, relief evident in my voice.

Lestrade carefully maneuvered his coat back on, with Holmes' assistance. He retrieved his hat from where it had fallen on the ground and dusted it off before returning it firmly to his head. "Thank you, Holmes. I owe both you and Doctor Watson my life."

Lestrade looked across to where angry shouts and swearing were emanating from the police wagon. The young sergeant saw Lestrade looking and came across. "I've arrested him for assault on you, sir. Do you want us to wait until you've been through the premises, or take him back now? If we wait, there will be fewer of us to come in with you. I reckon the bugger will scarper if we leave him unguarded in the wagon."

"Leave three of your men to guard Watkins," Holmes said. "I think seven of us are sufficient to take down a murderer. Even if he is armed with a knife, and Lestrade down the use of an arm." He walked away to inspect the front of the building.

The sergeant gave Lestrade an enquiring look. Lestrade nodded. "Holmes is right."

Lestrade gestured towards the front of the building. "Shall we, gentlemen?"

"Let the sergeant and his men go first," I said. "I do not think you should be breaking down any doors with that shoulder for a while."

Holmes was bent over, poking around the stone frontage of the building. "No one will be breaking down any doors today." Holmes straightened up and turned to us, holding up a door key for us to see.

"Where did you get that?" I asked.

"It was stuffed in a crack between two bricks. I saw the light reflect off it when we first arrived. Someone needs to explain to Mr. Croft the dangers of leaving keys where strangers can find them."

"I shall endeavor to give him that lecture, Mr. Holmes, right after I arrest him for murder," Lestrade replied acidly.

Holmes walked up the steps and tested the door. It was locked. He inserted the key into the lock, before looking over his shoulder to make sure we were with him. The young sergeant and I stood directly behind him. The remaining constables stood with Lestrade, slightly behind us.

Holmes turned the key in the lock, and carefully opened the door.

I peered over Holmes shoulder into the tidy little shop front. Bolts of worsted cloth sat neatly on a counter. A measuring tape lay coiled beside them. All seemed to be quiet and orderly. Dust motes danced in a sunbeam that the opening of the door had let in. All was silence. It appeared that there was no one was at home.

A quick look around the rear work area showed all was quiet and well-tended. A half-finished hunting coat sat wrapped around a tailor's dummy. Short black threads dangled from it. Holmes cast a quick eye around the room before pointing at the dark, narrow, staircase at the rear of the room. He placed a finger to his lips to signal quiet, and then pointed upwards. If our quarry was here, then he must be upstairs.

I attempted to move quietly up the stairs. Holmes loped ahead like a gazelle, leaving both Lestrade and I to glare resentfully after him. The young sergeant was at Holmes' heels. Halfway up the stairs I heard a door open, followed by Holmes' voice raised in anger.

Lestrade and I looked at each other, then gave up on attempting to be quiet, and hurried up the stairs to join Holmes.

Reaching Holmes' side, I looked through the door to a scene of what appeared, at first glance, to be destruction. Papers, scraps of cloth, clothing, and assorted bric-a-brac, littered the floor.

"It seems that our little bird has flown the nest, Watson," Holmes observed sourly.

Lestrade turned to the constables coming up behind us. "Look carefully, lads. With luck we will find something to tell us where he has gone."

Holmes sniffed. "Luck does not enter into the equation, Lestrade. You, of all people, should know that."

"Most of the time we get results from sheer hard work; occasionally, it is just bloody good luck," Lestrade retorted.

I ignored what was about to become a round of snapping and snarling, knowing that it was frustration on the part of both men, rather than any real disagreement.

The flat was not large. It consisted of one decent sized room, about the size of our sitting room at Baker Street, with the door in one wall and a window in the opposite one. To the right of the doorway a bed had been placed against that wall, with a small nightstand sitting on a rag rug beside it, on which reposed a washing bowl and jug. A glint of porcelain under the bed signaled the presence of a chamber pot. At the end of the bed sat a blanket box, no doubt containing Croft's clothing and any spare bedding he might have owned.

Beneath the window sat a small table with a single chair. A small loaf of bread sat on a board, covered with a piece of muslin cloth. Next to the table sat a small, somewhat shabby, walnut sideboard with plates displayed on it. Its closed doors no doubt containing shelves with cups, glasses and cutlery.

Along the other wall sat a small set of shelves containing what appeared to be pattern books and a small stack of periodicals. One shelf caught my eye. It was out of step with the neatly arranged papers on the other shelves. This one held a jumble of books and bric-a-brac. It was this shelf that had overflowed onto the floor giving the room its wretched appearance. At right angles to the shelves was a comfortable looking armchair and an oak side table.

I wandered around the little space, intent on ignoring the squabble going on behind me. A flash of gold on the floor caught my eye, tucked up against the edge of the sideboard. I bent down and retrieved the item. I stared at it for a long time, then turned to where Holmes and Lestrade were standing near the shelves, still eyeing each other like a pair of prize fighting cocks. Absently, I noticed that the uniformed officers were also ignoring them. No doubt well used to arguing detectives by now.

I cleared my throat. Both men turned to look at me.

"If you have both quite finished venting hot air..."

"What is it, Watson?" Holmes' tone was nowhere near as testy as I expected it to be.

"I think we can safely say that Nathaniel Croft has gone from possible suspect to definite."

"What makes you say that?" asked Lestrade.

I held out my find towards them. It was a scrap of green damask silk, with gold lace attached. It was the lace that had caught the light, causing it to gleam. It was definitely the same lace that young Daisy had torn from off the dress of her killer.

Holmes took it from me. "Oh, well done, Watson," he almost purred.

"Well done, indeed," added Lestrade.

My small find seemed to jolt Holmes from his angry funk, and he started methodically searching the flat. Feeling that I would only be in the way, and, I admit, feeling a little smug about my find, I stood in the doorway and watched the proceedings.

Lestrade joined me. With Holmes and the constables all searching, any more people and everyone would be tripping over each other.

"Not a very sociable man, our Mr. Croft," Lestrade commented.

I looked around the room. "Ah yes. Only one chair at the table and one to relax in. To be fair, it is a fairly small room."

Lestrade shrugged. "My room is about the same size and I have two armchairs."

"Do you have many visitors?" I asked.

Lestrade shrugged again. "Not as many as I would like," he admitted. For a moment I caught a glimpse of his loneliness. This was a man who had as few friends as Holmes and myself. We should entertain him more, I decided. After all, Lestrade was closer to me than any almost any other man of my acquaintance, apart from Holmes, and as I had recently discovered, Lestrade had the sort of dry wit that we both appreciated.

We both watched Holmes digging through the untidy pile on the shelf that I had noticed before. He was opening each book and flicking through it before discarding it on the floor. His eyes settled on a small, leather-bound notebook, similar to the ones I used for notes on cases. Holmes picked it up and examined the cover closely, then he opened it. A small smile crossed his face as he read the contents. Shutting the book, he walked across to join Lestrade and I at the door.

Holmes waved the book at us. "This may be what solves the case."

Lestrade blinked at him. "It is a notebook."

"Trenchant observation, Lestrade."

"A leather-bound notebook," I added, not really seeing exactly what it was that was exciting Holmes' attention.

Holmes held the book out for our mutual inspection. I noted that the leather cover was embossed with the initials M.C. I looked at Holmes, "It belonged to Michael Croft?"

"I believe so Watson, and I believe that what is inside is the key to the entire case."

Lestrade took the book from Holmes and opened it. "It does not make any sense!"

I looked over his shoulder at the open book. The penmanship was excellent, but the writing indeed made no sense, being a jumble of letters. I looked again at Holmes. "A code?"

"Well done, Watson. It is indeed a code."

Lestrade sighed. "I had best get this to the Yard and get someone working on trying to break it."

"There is no need to take it to the Yard," I told him. "Let Holmes have it. He is a highly skilled cryptographer."

Lestrade looked at the book in his hands for a moment, then handed it back to Holmes. "Take it. See what you can get from it. Meanwhile, I will see what we can do to track down where Nathaniel has gone to ground."

Holmes nodded and tucked the book into his pocket of his coat then he and I turned and left the flat, leaving Lestrade and his men to their search.

We walked from Marylebone High Street to Baker Street in silence. I could see that the problem of the coded notebook was already beginning to occupy my friend's mind, so I refrained from starting a conversation. Instead, I wondered where Nathaniel Croft had gone. I had a moment's panic as I wondered if he had gone to his sister's home, then I remembered the police officer that Lestrade had appropriated to watch over the women.

Holmes looked at me from the corner of his eye. "No need to worry, my friend. That young constable will see him off if he turns up at his sister's home."

I laughed ruefully. "My face gave me away again."

"It did indeed." He smiled slyly. "Stick to betting on the horses, my friend, because if you took up cards, you would lose everything you possessed."

"Why do you think I stick to the horses?"

In a slightly lighter mood, we continued home to Baker Street.

Once in our rooms, Holmes dropped the notebook on his desk, gathered paper and pens, sat down, and turned his complete attention to the job at hand. Knowing him as I did, I was aware that my presence could easily become a distraction, so I elected to go for a stroll in Regent's Park.

Chapter Sixteen

I returned from my walk several hours later to find Holmes still busy at his desk, but the atmosphere of the room thick with pipe smoke. Coughing slightly, I hastened to open the windows to clear the air. Holmes shot me a mildly irritated look.

"You may not see the need to breathe," I told him, "But I certainly do."

Holmes looked down at his pipe and his now nearly empty Persian slipper. "My deepest apologies, my friend. I had not realized how much I was smoking. It is very easy to lose track when immersed in a task like this."

"Have you broken the code?" I asked.

Holmes waved a hand in a dismissive gesture. "Several hours ago. I have now almost completed translating and transcribing the contents."

I noted the piles of paper littering his desk. "Has it been worthwhile?"

Holmes looked thoughtful. "Yes, I do believe it has."

"Will you tell me?"

Holmes shook his head. "No. I would rather not do this more than once. I believe that the best idea would be to arrange a meeting."

"With Lestrade?"

"And also, with Mycroft and Sir Lucas. There is much in this notebook that concerns everyone involved. Will you arrange for a telegram to Mycroft? Ask him to arrange the meeting and let us know when."

"Of course." I turned to go back downstairs.

Holmes sighed. "This is not going to end well."

I turned back. "It is not like you to make predictions."

"It is not a prediction. It is an inevitability, based on the contents of this journal. Michael Croft was not a happy man, and I understand, to a certain extent, why Nathaniel Croft is acting as he is. And I will tell you something else."

"What is that, Holmes?"

"Mycroft is going to be a very unhappy man."

"That will make a change."

My weak sally drew a low chuckle, devoid of humour, from my friend. It was evident that the contents of the journal were weighing heavily on his mind. I hastened away to complete my task.

The next morning a note came from Mycroft requesting us to attend a meeting at the Diogenes Club that afternoon.

We arrived at the Diogenes Club to find Sir Lucas already there with a slim young man, whose presence puzzled me for a moment, until I realized it was Dorothy in male garb. I had become so used to Dorothy that I had almost forgotten that I had originally met her as Daniel at the beginning of this dreadful case. Indeed, the very image of Daniel had been replaced in my mind with that of Dorothy.

Mycroft was seated in a large, comfortable chair, looking very uncomfortable every time he looked at Dorothy. He was trying extremely hard to ignore her very existence and failing. It occurred to me that a person such as Dorothy had probably never crossed his path before. Mycroft was operating far from his own realm of understanding.

Holmes, standing next to me, snorted his derision at his brother's palpable discomfort.

I looked around. "Lestrade is not here yet?"

Mycroft shook his head. "The inspector sent a message. He has been slightly delayed. Something to do with the case. I am sure he will share it with us in due course. Meanwhile, may I offer you coffee, Doctor Watson, Sherlock?"

Sir Lucas, who was sitting beside Dorothy, rose from his chair with a slight smile, and shook first Holmes' hand and then my own. "A pleasure to see both of you again. I was intrigued by your note, Mr. Holmes." This was addressed to Sherlock not Mycroft. "Suggesting that I bring Dorothy with me to the meeting."

Mycroft was regarding at his brother with all the sharp intensity of a cat deprived of its lawful kill.

"When did you send a note to Sir Lucas?" I murmured.

"When you went to send the telegram to Mycroft. I dispatched Wiggins."

"I am surprised Wiggins is not here as well."

"There are only so many shocks a man can take in one day, Watson. I feared Wiggins may have been one shock too many."

I sat down and began to chat amiably with Sir Lucas and Dorothy. Mycroft sat in his chair glowering indiscriminately at everyone, whilst Holmes prowled the room. It was obvious neither brother was happy with having to await the arrival of Lestrade.

Eventually, footsteps outside the door heralded Lestrade's appearance. He bustled through the door, quietly apologizing for his tardiness as he did so.

Mycroft waved a hand airily. "It is quite all right, Inspector. Your messenger said the delay was related to our meeting."

"It was." Lestrade sank heavily into one of the remaining chairs. Holmes finally taking the other one.

"Where do we want to start?" Lestrade asked.

"With the mysterious journal?" I suggested.

"A good idea, Doctor," said Mycroft. "Well, Sherlock?"

"The journal belonged to Michael Croft, as Watson surmised. He fancied himself as something of a Samuel Pepys."

Lestrade muttered something about defecation and fireplaces, which caused Sir Lucas to snort with amusement, and which Holmes chose to ignore.

"Samuel Pepys? Because he worked for the government?" asked Dorothy.

"Partly. Though perhaps Giacomo Casanova would be a more accurate comparison."

"You mean the journal details his…" Lestrade's voice trailed off. It was obvious that, like myself, he viewed Daniel as Dorothy even when she was in male garb. He obviously did not wish to be crude in front of her.

Holmes rolled his eyes. "Exactly, Lestrade." He looked across at Dorothy. "You will, I pray, excuse me if I am blunt?"

"Of course, Mr. Holmes." She smiled reassuringly at Lestrade. "You forget who Gertrude and I have been trying to get off the streets. I am sure the language you gentlemen use will not be in any way as rough as what I have heard others use before."

Holmes inclined his head in acknowledgement of Dorothy's observation. He turned to Mycroft. "Your vetting process for agents needs work."

Mycroft frowned. "Are you saying the Michael Croft was untrustworthy?"

"Not in and of himself, but his unfortunate predilections made him so."

"Do not beat about the bush, Holmes," Lestrade interjected. "Just tell us."

"As I was saying," Holmes' tone damn near had icicles dripping from it. "Michael Croft's journal is a diary of deception and vice. He deceived you, Mycroft, and his sister and brother-in-law at the very least, as to his upstanding character. As for vice…" Holmes looked down, distaste marring his features momentarily, before he composed them back into his usual mask. "Croft did not like women. His journal states as much. Indeed, at one point he is sneering of his own sister."

"When she discovered what he and Bradstreet were doing?" asked Lestrade.

Holmes nodded. "Michael Croft was a peculiar man. The most important person in his world was his brother Nathaniel."

"That makes some sense," I said thoughtfully, "the bond between twins is often much stronger than that between ordinary siblings."

"Indeed. I have read something of that. Michael Croft was decidedly peculiar in his private habits as well." Holmes waved the journal at us. "In this book he detailed his sexual congress with young whores like Nancy and Daisy. He exclusively used whores of that ilk. In his journal he rants on about female whores and dilly boys in a manner that is decidedly unhinged. He also sings the praises of his 'girls' as being far superior to either of the others. At least, up until a certain point."

Holmes fell silent.

It was Sir Lucas who broke the silence. "And that point was?"

"The point where he contracted syphilis from one of his 'girls.' After that, the later entries are a rant against everyone. Including Mrs. Swindon whom he had seen on the streets and assumed was a bawd." Holmes looked at Mycroft. "You need to train your men better. Croft's deduction skills were deplorable. He saw Mrs. Swindon talking to Daisy on Piccadilly and on the simple strength of that single instance decided that she was in charge of the girls."

Holmes looked down at the journal in his hand. "It becomes clear, while reading this, that Croft, while attracted to young men, was deeply ashamed of it, and so consorted with and used vulnerable young men who desperately wanted to be women."

"Mickey was popular," Dorothy said softly. "Molly said that he made her feel like a princess. That just for a short while she could forget the body, she was born in. He bought her ribbons, and flowers, and made her, and the other girls, feel special. The reality is however, that whatever finery you dress him in, Michael Croft was nothing more than a man who used whores."

"Apart from Daisy," Lestrade asked, "did he mention any other girls?"

Holmes nodded. "He mentions Nancy, and Molly as well as Daisy…and also one other. A girl he calls Antoinette. She is the one he believed gave him syphilis."

Lestrade jotted the name down in his notebook. "I will get someone to try and find her. If she is still alive, she may very well be in danger."

"Very much so," agreed Holmes. "Michael Croft's last entry in the journal states his intent to commit suicide after receiving the diagnosis. In that entry he states his belief that he contracted the disease from Antoinette."

Holmes flipped the journal open to show us other entries. They were in a different handwriting from Michael Croft's, but obviously in the same code.

"These later entries were made by Nathaniel. In them he states his intent to kill those he believed caused his brother's death. He listed the names of the girls and where they plied their trade. He also names Mrs. Swindon, and much later Dorothy and Archie's names appear in the book, along with that of Sir Lucas'."

Holmes looked at his brother. "It is obvious from the entries that Jeremiah came across Nathaniel while he was hunting. Jeremiah recognized the dress Croft was wearing as one belonging to his wife. He accosted Croft, believing, at first, that he was simply a receiver of stolen goods, but then Jeremiah saw Croft's face."

Mycroft bowed his head. "And for Nathaniel Croft to keep his secret, Jeremiah had to die."

"Yes."

"Sherlock."

"Yes, Mycroft?"

"Rest assured that Viola Bradstreet will want for nothing. I owe her much more than the paltry sum that I gave her at Jeremiah's funeral."

It was something of a shock to hear Mycroft openly voice his intentions. I remembered how he had disliked being found out for assisting the Smythe family. This, however, was much more than an avowal of intention. It was an admission that he had been in the wrong to employ, indeed to trust, a man such as Michael Croft had been.

Holmes looked at his brother for a moment in silence, then nodded once, and returned to his narrative.

"After the murder of Evelyn Smythe, the entries become a lot more erratic and disjointed."

"He fell apart when he discovered he had killed the wrong woman, just as we surmised," Lestrade said softly.

"Indeed. There is only one entry after the murder of Daisy. It simply reads: I have lost. I am lost." Holmes' expression was sour. "We have no way of knowing what his next move will be."

"He has already made one move that has been thwarted," Lestrade said.

We all looked at him. "That is one of the reasons that I was late. Croft tried to get at Archie."

Holmes' face, and Dorothy's, were horrified, and I am sure mine was not any better. Lestrade raised his hands. "Archie is all right. Croft tried to snatch him when Archie was walking Halliday's enormous dog."

"Tried?" There was a glimmer of a smile on Holmes' face, as if he had realized where this story was going.

"Tried," Lestrade said firmly. "The dog was not having any of it. It sank its teeth firmly into Croft's arse, pardon my language, ma'am." This was addressed to Dorothy who was having difficulty keeping a broad grin off her face.

"Halliday came to me with both Archie and the dog. The dog was not prepared to let go of its prize." Lestrade grinned viciously, "A bloodstained hunk of cloth from Croft's trousers. I had to send one of the constables out to the nearest butchers to get a nice slab of beef before the animal would give up its trophy."

"Have you alerted the hospitals about a possible dog bite case coming in?" asked Sir Lucas.

"Of course."

"Croft may have gone to a druggist or even his sister for help," said Mycroft.

"He will get a nasty surprise if he goes to his sister," I said. "That is if the constable is still there."

"He is," said Lestrade, "Or another of his colleagues. I made sure of it"

Mycroft raised his eyebrows enquiringly.

"Viola Bradstreet realized her other brother was a murderer when I showed her the button and lace, we got from Daisy's hand," Holmes admitted. "Lestrade arranged with the police at Putney to watch over her. When we left, there was a large constable ensconced in the house. Nathaniel Croft will get a very unpleasant welcome if he tries to impose upon his sister."

Mycroft was silent for a moment. "Good," was all he finally said.

"Where is Archie now?" Dorothy asked

"At A Division with Sergeant Halliday, being feted as a brave lad by the men on duty and being shown the around the station. When I left, he was assisting one of the junior constables to make tea and was extremely proud of himself." Lestrade grinned at Holmes. "I think you have definitely lost an Irregular and I have gained a copper."

Holmes smiled briefly. "He will make a good one."

"Monro and Anderson came in while Archie was explaining to a large group of enthralled coppers how the dog bit Croft and how he had personally kicked Watkins in the shins for hitting a lady," said Lestrade.

"Their reactions must have been interesting," Sir Lucas observed in the tones of one who has met both men and found them wanting.

Lestrade grinned again. "I admit I expected trouble. But I have to give both men their dues. They sat down, listened to Archie tell his story, again, with every evidence of being deeply interested in what happened. After Archie had finished, they both told him he was a brave and clever lad and would be an asset to the Metropolitan Police when the time came and left.

Not before Anderson gave him a small packet of humbugs, and Monro slipped him a shilling."

"Lestrade is right, Holmes, you have most definitely lost an Irregular," I said with a small laugh.

"It is very hard for Sherlock to compete with a packet of humbugs," Mycroft agreed with a smile. He turned to Lestrade. "You said this was one reason you were late. That implies there is another."

"I have been having a nice long chat with the now former Constable Watkins."

"Did Watkins have anything of interest to share with you?" Holmes asked.

"Watkins went to school with the Croft twins. He was close to them. Well, as close as one can get to twins who do everything together. Nathaniel came to him after Michael's death looking for help. Watkins did not take much persuading to assist."

"What form did this assistance take?" asked Sir Lucas.

"He tracked the victims for Nathaniel. Found their favoured places to solicit. Watched the Cleveland Street house for him. That sort of thing."

"How did he find the house?" asked Dorothy.

"Police records after Mrs. Swindon was arrested for running a brothel. Naturally, the address was in the records. Not hard for him to get at it whilst allegedly looking for something else."

"But he took no part in the killings?" asked Mycroft.

"No. He was careful to be elsewhere. Watkins may have known what was going on, but obviously felt that being present at a murder or two was a step too far."

"He equally obviously had no qualms when it came to arson," Sir Lucas observed.

"Watkins claims to have known nothing about that. He says Nathaniel told him keep watch on the house when he could. He claims he arrived that evening after the fire was lit. His instructions were that if he spotted Mrs. Swindon to send for Nathaniel at once. I do not think it occurred to either man that she could be living with you in Kensington. Watkins kept visiting Cleveland Street hoping to spot her."

"I am surprised he did not try to get to us both at my Kensington house," Sir Lucas remarked.

Lestrade shook his head. "According to Watkins, Nathaniel thought about it. But decided it was too much of a risk."

"What was Watkins doing at the Marylebone address?" I asked.

"He had come to check on Nathaniel. As he had not heard from him for a couple of days and was starting to worry. At least, that is his story."

"You suspect differently?" Mycroft asked.

"He was carrying his truncheon. That does imply that he had other things in mind," said Lestrade.

"Like the attempted murder of a Scotland Yard inspector," I said.

"Like that, yes."

"Watkins tried to kill you?" Mycroft asked.

"Yes, Mr. Holmes. Foiled by your brother and by Doctor Watson."

"We have our uses, eh, Watson?" Holmes said with a slight smile.

"Occasionally, Holmes, very occasionally," I replied.

"That is basically it," said Lestrade. "Watkins had nothing more to tell us. He was more concerned with shouting imprecations at myself and the arresting officers." Lestrade looked around at us all. "The question is, what do we do now?"

"A valid question, Inspector, and the reason for our meeting," said Mycroft.

Holmes frowned. "I had hoped to persuade Watkins to act as our messenger to Croft."

Lestrade shook his head. "That is not going to work for two reasons. One: he genuinely does not seem to know where Croft is. Two: I am pretty sure hell will freeze over before he deigns to do favours for either you or me. He tried to kill me, and you nearly broke his arm stopping him from doing so."

"Should have broken his neck," I muttered.

"It would be a little difficult to get him to talk if he were dead, Doctor Watson," observed Mycroft. "Not unless you hold one of those séances that have been taking society by storm."

"So, what do we do to drag Croft out of whatever hidey-hole he has inserted himself into?" I asked.

"I could lure him out," Dorothy said softly. All eyes turned to her. "Remember, Croft saw me when he killed Daisy."

Holmes frowned. "I am not sure that is a good idea. He is a strong man who has already overpowered and killed six people. I would not like you to be the seventh."

"Let us not be in too much of a hurry to write off the idea," Mycroft said. "If we can arrange it so there are watchers close by who can intervene, we can minimize the risk to…" Mycroft paused, then said, "… this young person."

Sir Lucas just looked slightly pained, and Dorothy wearily accepting, of Mycroft's attitude.

"Are we sure there is no way we can use Watkins to draw out Nathaniel?" I asked. Mycroft's attitude was annoying me, and I also did not want to put Dorothy in danger.

"Lestrade is correct" Holmes said. "Watkins has no reason to co-operate with us."

Lestrade frowned. "I can think of one."

"And what is that?" asked Mycroft.

"If someone has a word to Monro and gets his agreement, we may be able to persuade him to drop the charges against Watkins if he will help us."

"Excellent idea," said Mycroft. "I will talk with Monro personally and see what we can arrange. We shall convene here again tomorrow at the same time."

We all took our leave and returned to our respective abodes, hopeful of what the next afternoon would bring.

Chapter Seventeen

"Monro was reluctant to assist," Mycroft told us the next afternoon, "but I managed to persuade him of the value of the idea."

Lestrade sighed. "Valuable or not, it did not work."

"Watkins will not cooperate?" asked Sir Lucas.

"No. In fact, he was rather graphic in his descriptions of what we could do with our suggestion. Anderson was outraged, and when I left, he was busy trying to work out just how many things Watkins could be charged with."

"So, unless we can come up with another idea, then the only suggestion we have to work on is Dorothy's," said Sir Lucas.

"Perhaps Sherlock's guttersnipe might be a more acceptable alternative? After all, he saw Nathaniel Croft as well," said Mycroft.

I am not sure Mycroft was expecting the level of fury that was directed at him. Holmes opened his mouth to speak but was beaten to it by an extremely irate Dorothy.

"That 'guttersnipe' has a name, if you bothered to learn it, Mr. Holmes. Archie is a brave, intelligent, boy and will make an excellent police officer someday. You will not endanger him. I forbid it!"

Mycroft gaped at her. He looked around as if for support, catching Lestrade's eye, but the inspector showed only a cold-eyed countenance with mouth set in a disapproving line. Sir Lucas' expression was equally disapproving.

"The reality is," Dorothy continued, "that the only worthwhile bait you have is me. I have volunteered."

"As reluctant as I am to put Dorothy into the path of danger," Holmes said quietly, "she is correct."

"How shall we do this?" asked Sir Lucas.

"Our major difficulty is getting a message to Nathaniel Croft. If we knew where he is, we would not need to go through this," said Holmes.

"Where? When? How?" asked Lestrade, summing every possible question up succinctly.

"The Embankment, do you think, Mycroft?" asked Holmes.

Mycroft nodded. "Near the Westminster Bridge. It should resonate for him. He has killed there before, and it is also where Michael committed suicide. As for when, there is a full moon in two weeks. Plenty of light, but also plenty of shadows for the concealment of police officers. As for contacting him…"

"Advertisements in all the papers. We state the date of the last murder and its whereabouts. Hint strongly enough that the advertiser has information for sale, and, for his own safety, Nathaniel should take the bait," said Holmes.

Lestrade got to his feet. "If you gentleman want to draft up the advertisement, I will get back to the Yard. I need to speak to my superiors about the man-power for this little fishing expedition."

"Monro promised full co-operation," I reminded him. "I do not think either he or Anderson will take too much convincing."

Lestrade nodded and took his leave, while the rest of us settled in to work out the wording of the advertisements and plan the main details of the trap.

Mycroft undertook to see the advertisement prominently placed in all the newspapers and we all took our leave. There was really nothing now for us to do but wait for the appointed night. I feared that Holmes would grow restless, but it seemed that the approaching finale was enough to keep him alert and stimulated for those two long weeks.

The night of the full moon found us rugged up against the cold and lurking in the vicinity of Westminster Bridge. Dark clouds scudded across the sky, obscuring then revealing the moon, leaving the area awash with dancing shadows. A chill mist was slowly seeping up from the river, swirling around our ankles, and adding to the feeling of unreality that encompassed the scene.

Holmes and I waited in the shadows on the river stairs, close enough to where Dorothy stood under a lamp at the Parliament end of the bridge. She was positioned so that we could reach her quickly.

Mycroft had remained at the Diogenes Club, saying that a man of his bulk had no business dashing around in the dark catching criminals. Sir Lucas had remained with him.

Lestrade slipped down the stairs to join us. "Everyone is in position," he said quietly. "I have men in plainclothes watching all northern approaches to the bridge."

Waiting is the most tedious part of any occupation. Waiting in the shadows with the cold air from the Thames playing around us, was probably the most tedious wait I had endured since my return to London. My shoulder was beginning to ache, when we realized something was wrong. A figure was approaching Dorothy from the southern end of the bridge. Lestrade swore softly.

Holmes' tone dripped acid. "You have men only on the northern approach to the bridge."

Dorothy heard the footsteps and began to turn, placing her back against the wall of the bridge. Light reflected off the blade of a knife held by the figure who now had Dorothy pinned and helpless.

With a cry of anger, I raced up the steps and ran towards the armed figure, who turned when he heard me and lunged in my direction with the knife. I dodged out of the way but slipped on the damp ground and fell heavily on my side. I twisted on my back and tried to rise, but as I did so, I saw the blade of the knife begin to descend. Distantly I could hear Holmes and Lestrade's voices and rapidly approaching footsteps. Behind me I heard the sound of a police whistle being blown with some urgency.

There was a shriek of pain, and my assailant staggered away. The knife he had been holding clattered to the ground. He was shaking his hand and swearing. Blood drops flew from his hand, splattering onto the ground beside me. Dorothy stood at bay, a knife clutched in her own hand. The brave lass had slashed the killer's left hand open to the bone. He had had to drop the knife to try and staunch the bleeding. As he staggered under the street lamp, it became clear that the attacker was indeed Nathaniel Croft.

Shrieking curses, he lurched towards Dorothy, both arms outstretched as if to throttle the life out of her, blood flowing from his injured hand. A gun barked and Nathaniel staggered back, using his damaged left hand to clutch at his right shoulder where he had been winged.

Holmes helped me to my feet. To my left I saw Lestrade, gun in hand, approaching Nathaniel. Dorothy stood safely behind Lestrade, knife still clutched in her hand; fire and fury in her eyes.

The constables gathered at the end of the bridge. Unwilling to get between the armed inspector and his prey, and even more unwilling to approach the equally dangerous young lady with the knife.

Nathaniel turned towards Holmes and myself. His face a mask of deranged fury. "Damn you to hell, you interfering bastards. Those deviant bitches deserved to die. Giving my brother that foul disease."

"What is your excuse for murdering your brother-in-law?" Lestrade snapped.

"Or the totally innocent widow, Evelyn Smythe?" I added just as sharply.

A shadow crossed Nathaniel's face. "I am sorry about the widow," he admitted. "And I really am sorry about having to kill Jeremiah. But I had not finished my cleansing of the city, and he would have stopped me."

"Well, you are stopped now," Lestrade said. "Nathaniel Croft, I arrest you for the murders of Evelyn Smythe, Jeremiah Bradstreet, Thomas Arbuthnot, Daisy Macklin, Molly

Clutterbuck and the whore known only as Nancy, not to mention the arson attack on the Cleveland Street house."

Lestrade had been moving slowly towards Croft, who had been moving with equal slowness towards the side of the bridge. Croft smiled bitterly at Lestrade's words, and then laughed. The hair on the back of my neck rose at the sound. It was chilling, mirthless, and completely devoid of sanity.

"I do not think so. I will see you bastards in Hell!" With that, Croft threw himself over the edge of the bridge and into the fast-flowing Thames below. Holmes, Dorothy, and I ran to the side of the bridge and looked over. There was no sign of Croft. Behind us, I could hear Lestrade yelling for someone to organize a boat. Even as he yelled, I knew he was wasting his time. Nathaniel Croft had gone the way of his brother.

Chapter Eighteen

It was late the following day before we could meet again at the Diogenes Club. This time, Dorothy was present as her true self, which must have given the more curmudgeonly members of the club something to really grumble about. I watched with amusement as Mycroft graciously poured tea for Dorothy, with no sign of his previous discomfort. I wondered what had happened to change him. Holmes saw me watching and gave a sly smile. "My brother has finally learned that being female does not mean being incompetent. It was bound to happen eventually."

Much to my surprise Monro and Anderson were also present. They sat beside Sir Lucas, all three of them drinking tea and discussing France. I remembered that Anderson was fond of the country, having been virtually dragged back from there during the Ripper case.

Lestrade sat beside Holmes, gazing morosely into his cup. It was obvious that Lestrade was still unhappy about Croft evading capture, even if it did mean the man was dead. I also knew, that like myself and Holmes, Lestrade would be wary and alert until Croft's corpse was discovered.

Monro put down his cup and smiled briefly. "A good result gentleman, and lady." He inclined his head towards Dorothy, who acknowledged his address with a slight nod. "A good result even if we have no-one to charge."

"You have someone to charge," Holmes said.

"And who would that be?" Monro asked.

"Watkins, of course," Holmes snapped. "Or are you going to let him get away with that murderous attack on Lestrade?"

Monro looked uncomfortable. Anderson looked away. It was obvious to me that the two men had had a disagreement on the subject.

"You are not going to let him off, I trust?" My tone held a level of ice that surprised even me.

"The reputation of the force…" Monro bleated.

"Letting an ex-police officer get away with attempted murder, not to mention abetting a confessed murderer is hardly good publicity for the London Metropolitan Police." Holmes tone was as frigid as my own.

"I have a suggestion," said Mycroft. "A way out of this that both keeps the reputation of the police intact and punishes Watkins."

Holmes looked at his brother, eyebrows arching upwards in enquiry.

"Cecil Rhodes is putting together a force under the auspices of the British South Africa Company to attempt to take control of Mashonaland and Matebeleland before the Germans can get their hands on them. Offer this Watkins the choice of joining this force or facing time in prison. I am sure he will see reason." Mycroft gave a wintry smile. "He is not a trained soldier, so the odds are extremely high that he will not return from the expedition. I can also guarantee that he will be accepted as a member of the force."

"Pray remind me never to get on your brother's bad side," Lestrade murmured softly to Holmes.

Monro looked around at everyone. "Well, that ties up everything nicely."

"Not quite everything," said Sir Lucas. "Mother, grandmother, Gertrude, and I are moving to France. France is a more accepting place and I think we will all be comfortable there. Mr. Holmes, Doctor Watson, Inspector Lestrade, I extend to you a standing invitation to come and stay with us. I have purchased a small chateau outside of Paris. David and his family will move into the Kensington house. I am selling the Cleveland Street property. I believe I will be far happier and certainly feel much safer away from Britain. Mycroft tells me there are dangerous changes coming."

"What about Dorothy?" I asked. I looked across to where the lady was seated near Mycroft.

Dorothy smiled. "I will not be going with Sir Lucas."

A look of concern crossed Holmes's face. "My dear lady, are you sure you will be safe alone in London?"

"Do not worry Sherlock," Mycroft said with a slight smile. "I have given much thought to your suggestion as to the hiring of female agents. Miss Watts will be working at Imperial Exports ostensibly as a type-writer. But given her bravery and intelligence, she will actually be one of my agents. The American Pinkerton Agency has female agents after all."

"God forbid that we should allow the Americans to do anything better than us," said Lestrade, with a completely straight face.

"Exactly, Inspector."

"And Archie?" I asked.

Sir Lucas smiled. "Dorothy is concerned about the boy. I have arranged for his education to be paid for. Inspector Lestrade tells me he has a good home with one of his sergeants and his wife. He is a bright lad. A stable home and a good education will see him go far."

Monro laughed. "I would not be at all surprised if he ended up Commissioner of Police one day. The lad has a lot of promise."

So, with goodbyes and good wishes exchanged we left the Diogenes Club and returned to Baker Street.

I was sitting at my desk writing up my case notes a couple of days later when Lestrade arrived at our rooms. "He has been found," he said, as he walked in the door.

"Croft?" I asked.

Lestrade nodded. "Washed up at St. Katherine's Dock. At almost the exact same place as his brother did. River Police contacted me this morning."

"Does Mrs. Bradstreet know?" I asked.

"Yes," replied Lestrade, "As soon as I identified the body I went and told her. I think she is relieved, to be honest."

"The case is finally over," Holmes said.

Lestrade nodded again. "All loose ends tied up. We have found Antoinette as well. Born Anthony Burlestone. She died of syphilis in the Lock hospital about six months ago. The disease was far advanced when she passed it on to Michael Croft."

"Croft must have known long before he got the diagnosis that he had the pox. And he knowingly continued to use those girls. Even if Nathaniel had not murdered them, they would have lived much shortened, immensely painful, lives," I said. "The man was the worst sort of cad."

Holmes picked up his violin, walked to the window, and stared out at the street.

Lestrade and I exchanged a look. "Holmes?" I said softly.

"How many of them do you think there are, Watson?"

"How many what?"

"Poor unfortunates like that Antoinette? Like Molly. Like Nancy."

It was Lestrade who answered. "Too many. For every one that is accepted the way Dorothy has been, there are hundreds more thrown out of their homes by uncaring family to survive as best they can on the streets. And that best is often not enough."

The three of us stood for a moment, united in a sad silence.

Lestrade took his leave with a slight bow. I returned to my writing, with the melancholy sound of Holmes playing drifting around me.

AUTHOR'S NOTE

You way wonder at the way I have written Lestrade. I have long been fascinated by the way Lestrade's attitude towards Sherlock Holmes changed between "A Study in Scarlet" and "The Hound of the Baskervilles." There had to be a point where Lestrade went from being obstructive to actually liking Holmes enough to go well out of his jurisdiction to assist him as he did on Dartmoor. As for Lestrade's character, his response in "Hound" to Holmes' query as to whether or not he had his gun with him was: "As long as I have my trousers I have a hip-pocket, and as long as I have my hip-pocket I have something in it." A response that has always struck me as both whimsical and sarcastic.

Transgender people were treated appallingly by the Victorian establishment. Female to Male trans were more or less ignored or viewed as unfeminine hoydens. Male to Female trans were derisively referred to as "He/She Ladies" as I mentioned in the story. No real attempt was made by the medical profession to understand. Neil McKenna's book, "Fanny and Stella: The Young Men Who Shocked Victorian England," illustrates possibly the best-known case.
That book was the trigger for writing this story.

Another book I found incredibly useful was Ruth Goodman's "How to Be a Victorian." Assorted books by both Fergus Linnane, and Catharine Arnold were also consulted.

The references to a scandal brewing in Cleveland Street are based on fact. In the summer of 1889, there was a massive media explosion as it was revealed that a boy brothel was operating in Cleveland Street, staffed by mostly telegraph boys and frequented by members of the aristocracy. If you want to know more about it, the book "The Sins of Jack Saul" by Glenn Chandler, will be of interest.

Archie used the term "mutton shunter" to describe Constable Watkins. This was Victorian slang, a term of abuse really, for a certain type of policeman. One who was so low down in the pecking order that his job consisted of mostly moving prostitutes along from where they were plying their trade on the streets.

The title of this books is possibly slightly anachronistic. Males who dressed as women were known as "Mollies" in the 18th century, but the word does seem to have continued through into the Victorian era.

In 1893 New Zealand become the first country to give women the vote in Parliamentary elections.